Priscilla Asks Why?

Priscilla Asks Why?

The Rest of the Story

Written by
Janet Mary Sinke

An extended version of the children's picture book,
Priscilla McDoodleNutDoodleMcMae Asks Why?

Janet Mary Sinke
My Grandma and Me Publishers
P. O. Box 144
St. Johns, Michigan 48879

Website: www.mygrandmaandme.com
E-mail: janetmarysinke@gmail.com
or
info@mygrandmaandme.com

Cover design: Natalie Pennington
Illustrations: Craig Pennington

First Edition
Printed and bound in Ann Arbor, Michigan by Malloy

ISBN: 978-0-9742732-9-7

Dedicated to:
all those
whose hearts and souls
long for peace.

Contents

Part Two

Part Three

Part Six

Acknowledgements

To my husband, Mike, who renews my faith, frees me to explore all avenues in life, and encourages me to dream the impossible.

To my children, their spouses and all my grandchildren for they provide me with a special inspiration. They are the joys of my life.

To the good students at Scott Elementary in DeWitt, Michigan whose honest critique of this story helped to make its publication a reality.

To Craig and Natalie Pennington whose artistic talents help to enhance the written word.

Introduction

Once upon a time, in a place far away, there existed on the outer edge of the universe, a very large galaxy.

Spinning within this galaxy were trillions of cosmic bodies. There were colorful stars reflecting prisms of gorgeous light and fast comets with long, vaporizing tails. There were moons of all sizes orbiting precious planets where unique forms of life searched for their own sense of purpose, for everything is created for a reason.

And so it was for one tiny moon no bigger than a seed of a thistle. It floated in the blackness and was held in space, like all celestial bodies, by a strange magnetic force. And though many light years away, this moon was special because it looked very much like our own mother earth. It was blessed with many of the same gifts.

There were beautiful flowers and majestic trees that formed colorful landscapes while green, dense forests with their babbling brooks and streams provided havens for many interesting animals.

There was night, and there was day.

It was a peaceful place where many wonderful beings lived. These beings, like us, were basically good and kind folks till one day they suffered a terrible division.

It began with an argument between two very mixed up kings, and like most arguments that go on and on, each side believed its side and only its side was right. The kings closed their minds. They failed to listen and as time went on, respect was lost for all those who were considered different. This dangerous way of thinking soon spread, and it poisoned the minds and hearts of those who inhabited this tiny orb. The two kings' love of power and disrespect of others threatened to destroy all who lived there.

That is, till one day, one brave little girl dared to ask *Why?*

Part One

On a moon spinning round in a place far away

Lived Priscilla McDoodleNutDoodleMcMae

A girl who was common, considered quite shy

Till one day she questioned two kings with a Why?

1

Priscilla

It was a gorgeous morning. The sky was clear, the air clean. A quiet contentment filled the little cottage where Priscilla lived with her mother and father. Their house was the only house on the moon's faraway hill extending to the north. A clearing surrounded their dwelling, and a protective forest touched all sides of the clearing's outer edge. There were no roads that led in or out. Only one, narrow, well-hidden path provided a way to the outside world.

Priscilla had a habit of waking early. She loved the sights and sounds of morning especially after a good sleep, and so she started this day like any other, by quietly sitting outside on her swing, alone with her thoughts.

The swing hung from the only tree in her yard.

It was close to the cottage window which allowed Priscilla's parents to keep an attentive eye on her as they feared for their only daughter's safety. There were strict rules. She knew her boundaries. The clearing was as far as she could go.

Priscilla was small for her age, yet healthy. She had beautiful, green eyes and a sweet face. She was shy at times but a deep thinker who viewed life differently than most, and though Priscilla dressed and looked like other eleven-year-old girls her age, she was forced to wear one thing that made her different, a yellow bonnet.

It was an old-fashioned bonnet, or at least Priscilla thought so. It fit tight around her face to insure that every strand of her hair was covered. Her father especially insisted that Priscilla wear the bonnet at all times. And so, like a good daughter, she did as he requested. But that did not change one basic fact: Priscilla hated her bonnet.

On warm days it was hot and uncomfortable. It sometimes made her face sweat, especially around her hair line. She complained to her mother who convinced her father to free Priscilla of her bonnet at least when confined to her own home.

The young daughter understood her father's concern. She was different and he wanted to protect her. But on this beautiful, summer morning, as she swayed lazily on her swing, she thought about the unfairness of it all.

"*Why?*" she wondered out loud, "should it matter what I wear on my head? I'm a regular kid, aren't I? So what if my hair is different. *Why* am I alone? *Why* am I an outcast? It's not fair!" And suddenly she felt very sad as thoughts of unanswered *Whys* floated inside her head.

But Priscilla was not a girl who dwelled on negative issues for very long. She watched as fading stars of night bowed out to greet the dawn of day, and as she did so, her mood changed. She gave thanks for the magnificent sunrise and the beauty of the wood. She listened as baby birds called to their mothers who were busy digging up breakfasts in the dew-covered grass. Priscilla tried to imagine her own mother serving up an early meal of slimy worms and raw, crunchy bugs.

"Yuck!" Priscilla said out loud. "I'm glad I'm not a bird." Still, she enjoyed the sight of feathered mamas tending to their young. The morning was alive with all kinds of sights and sounds of nature.

Then, the clock tower chimed in the distance.

It was 7:00 a.m. She had one hour of quiet time left for precisely at 8:00 a.m. loudspeakers placed at strategic points around the little moon would activate for one hour. The speakers were meant to serve as a way for the moon's two kings to communicate on a daily basis with the good citizens of this land.

At first the loudspeakers seemed like a great idea. Both kings agreed to have a calm and peaceful discussion of various issues each morning between 8:00 a.m. and 9:00 a.m. But a major problem soon developed. The two kings grew to dislike each other intensely. Each one insisted that he was the wiser and therefore the most qualified to reign as sole ruler.

They judged themselves and every citizen by the color of their hair. King Norman ruled over all redheads while King Wynthor governed the blue. No other colors existed, or so they thought.

It wasn't long before the kings' early morning meetings became daily screaming matches. They called each other names and occasionally even slapped one another. Most of their time was spent declaring new laws that served no purpose except to benefit their own selfish needs.

But perhaps the most dangerous and frustrating of all their decrees was contained in one simple law that was strictly enforced. Simply stated, it was a law that prohibited anyone to pose a question to either king beginning with the word *Why*. Both Norman and Wynthor feared such questions could lead to a loss of power and so the *Why* word was stricken from all dictionaries and spelling books, indeed from their native language altogether. Eventually, any *Why* questions were forbidden even among the citizens themselves but that did not stop Priscilla from asking questions at least in her own mind.

She remembered in years past when the kings' threatening, high-pitched voices had frightened her. Now she found their routine arguments almost funny and rather entertaining. Their thinking and name-calling were, at least in Priscilla's mind, so ridiculous and so pointless that she couldn't help but laugh at times.

But on this particular beautiful morning Priscilla had no desire to listen to their royal majesties. She was bored with the kings' fighting and bickering. In fact she was pretty much bored with everything in her life right now.

"If only I had a friend," Priscilla thought.

She had yearned for someone for so long: someone with an understanding mind and a caring heart, someone who would listen, someone she could count on. In turn she longed to be such a friend to someone else. She continued to mull over these thoughts as she swayed on her swing.

"I need a change of scenery," Priscilla said to herself.

She smiled. She knew exactly where to go.

2

To the Forest

Priscilla rose quietly from her swing. She was very careful not to let it bang against the tree. Her parents were light sleepers, and she did not want to wake them. Slowly, she tiptoed to the cottage window.

Her eyes did a quick scan of the inside. Nope. Not up yet. Hopeful that her mother and father would remain sleeping for another hour, she continued to tiptoe across the clearing to the edge of the forest. She glanced back one last time before slipping into the trees and onto the hidden path which led to a large oak.

It was an old tree anchored by tough, gnarled roots. Priscilla had climbed the giant oak many times but only to the lower hanging limbs. She felt safe in its branches.

Now, as she stood at its base, it seemed as if the old tree were coaxing her to go higher, to explore, to see the world from a different angle. And so she began to climb, and as she did so she felt a confidence in her reach and a strength in her footing. She climbed higher. It seemed so easy.

Her excitement grew until an inside voice reminded Priscilla of the strict boundaries set by her parents. She did not like going against their wishes.

"But what's a girl to do?" she asked herself.

She stopped her ascent. Her nagging conscience persisted.

"Every kid needs a favorite place to go," Priscilla argued with herself. "I need a special place to think, a place to solve my own problems, a place where I can dare to ask *Why?*"

Her reasoning seemed to justify her actions so she resumed her climb going much higher than she had ever gone before.

She was nearly to the top when she came to a group of branches that formed a comfortable lookout. She nestled herself in among the leaves.

"The climb was worth it," she told herself. "Yes, this is the perfect spot."

From here Priscilla could see the fading morning mist and the castle towers stretching high into sunlit skies. She looked further across the tree lines and saw the beauty of the meadows. She found herself totally overwhelmed by the magnificent view.

Then, Priscilla looked down. It made her dizzy. She felt she might panic.

"*Don't look down. Don't look down.*" She repeated over and over.

She stared straight ahead and refocused.

"*Don't look down. Don't look down.*"

A quiet calm began to wash over her.

Priscilla smiled a contented smile for it was here in this place of quiet solitude where she felt a sense of freedom. It was here where gentle breezes cooled her face and filled her soul with peace, and it was here where she was about to meet her own destiny.

She closed her eyes and relaxed in the great oak's branches, her left leg gently swinging in the open space of the tree.

It wasn't long before she heard tapping on the bark in the branches above her.

3

Who's There?

Priscilla wasn't quite sure if she were dreaming or if
the trees swaying in the wind were merely playing
tricks on her. She pinched herself to make sure she
wasn't sleeping. Yup, she was awake all right. She
began to shake. She was afraid. The tapping on the
bark was rhythmic. It sounded like drumsticks, as if
someone were keeping beat to a modern day rock
song. Priscilla listened more intently.

"It's nothing more than a branch in the wind,"
she told herself, but when she heard a voice
singing, "*A-Bop-Bop-A Bee-Bop-A-Bop-Bop-A-Boo*"
she knew for certain that this was no branch in the
wind.

She reached to pull back the leaves, but fear
overcame her. She hesitated then called, instead, in
a weak, soft voice, "H-h-h-hello?"

12

The tapping stopped. All was quiet.

"H-h-h-hello," Priscilla repeated.

The leaves rustled.

"Excuse me," her voice sounded weak. "Is any-one there?"

No answer.

She went on, "I promise not to hurt you."

The leaves rustled again.

"Someone or something is in this tree with me," she thought.

She looked down. She was far too high to make a run for it. She waited, her heart beating faster.

"H-h-h-hello," she tried again.

Silence.

She had to know. Was it friend or foe?

"Only one way to find out," thought Priscilla.

She took a deep breath, reached forward and pulled back the branches.

4

The Fall

Priscilla gasped.

"Why, it's a baboon, a blue baboon!" She cried out.

The baboon was terrified. He held his self-carved drumsticks in one hand while clinging to the trunk of the magnificent tree with the other. His face was turned away from her. He was hanging on for dear life.

"*Don't look down. Don't look down.*" The baboon repeated over and over again.

Priscilla watched as he slowly turned his head. She opened her mouth to scream but no sound was there. Her eyes gazed in disbelief. She had never seen a blue baboon before.

"Very interesting," Priscilla said as she studied him more intensely.

She repositioned her feet on a crooked branch, standing now on tiptoe, in order to get a better look. He did not appear dangerous. She reached extending her hand in friendship. And as she did so, she felt her right foot slip.

Startled, Priscilla began to panic. She was losing her balance as she fought to hang on. "Help me, please!" Priscilla cried.

Her feet were struggling to find a foothold while her hands were clinging to a small branch just above her.

She implored him again, "Help me!"

Just then a squirrel with an acorn came out of the leaves and sat on the baboon's right shoulder. The baboon screamed at the small, furry-tailed creature causing it to run off in another direction. The baboon, startled by the squirrel's presence, dropped his drumsticks.

"Darn it all!" he yelled in frustration.

He thought about the little girl falling. Then, the snap of a branch—her branch.

The baboon shrieked. He blindly extended one hand, groping for Priscilla but then found himself losing his own grip, so he shrieked again while turning his face away from her. He couldn't bear to watch her tumble.

"*Don't look down. Don't look down.*"

The blue baboon shut his eyes and waited for a thump-like sound from the hard ground below. Instead he thankfully heard her voice call out again.

"Down here, Mr. Baboon. I'm down here." But the baboon would not look to where her voice was coming from.

"Please help me, whoever you are," pleaded Priscilla.

"I can't. I'm too afraid," he replied.

She could tell he was terrified.

"I need your help, Mr. Baboon," Priscilla said in a shaky voice. She, too, was terrified but knew she must remain calm. "I promise everything will turn out fine," she continued, "if we just work together. Now, if you could give me your hand, I'd really appreciate it."

The baboon slowly turned his head in her direction. He wanted to believe her.

He opened one eye.

He looked down.

He could see Priscilla dangling from a flimsy

branch in the open space of the tree. A drop from that height would mean certain death.

He opened his mouth and screamed again.

"Mr. Baboon," I don't think screaming is really going to help very much," Priscilla said in a shaky voice, "Please try and stay calm and don't panic! I repeat, don't panic!"

"What do you mean, don't panic!" The baboon fired back. "My gut is full of panic! I may even throw up or wet my fur! That's how panicked I am! So don't pressure me, kid, 'cause you're right in the line of fire!

"Oh, dear! I don't feel so good," he moaned.

"Great," Priscilla said to herself, "a blue baboon with an attitude." She did not want to agitate him further. She could tell he was somewhat high-strung.

"Mister Baboon," Priscilla reminded him, "you climbed up this tree, so I think it's very reasonable to assume that you can climb back down."

Her words did not convince him.

"Yeah, well that's before I discovered something very important about myself," the baboon told her.

"And what's that?" Priscilla hated to ask.

"What's what?" the baboon returned her question.

"What have you discovered?" Priscilla was losing her patience. "You just told me that you've made an important discovery about yourself." She reminded him.

"Oh yeah, my important discovery, well, you see Kid," he was stumbling for words. "I . . . well . . . I hate to be the one to tell you this, but I, uh . . . I have this phobia, you see, and I, uh . . . Well, it seems I have this tremendous fear of heights. I never knew this about myself till just now. So I hope you understand; as much as I would like to help you, I can't. Sorry."

His voice was shaking. He was ready to crack.

"Just my luck," Priscilla said to herself again, "a blue baboon who not only has an attitude, but a fear of heights as well."

She didn't have much time. Priscilla could feel her small branch slowly giving way. Panic was now building in her own mind. Her heart raced and her arm was growing weak as if it might pull out of its own socket. The baboon was her only hope.

She tried a different approach.

"Mr. Baboon, I want you to know that I have studied your species, and I have learned that baboons love trees. Did you know that? You climb trees all the time. You eat in trees. You sleep in trees, and you look out for possible trouble in trees."

"Well, I've certainly found trouble, that's for sure," the baboon answered back.

"And, uh, oh yeah, you love to swing from tree branch to tree branch using your special, gripping tail," she lied. "It's a basic instinct that you have. You do it very naturally. So saving me should be an easy task for you if you stop and think about it."

"There's just one problem, Kid," the baboon answered, "I've never swung from a tree branch in my life! I was taken from the jungle when I was very young. I lived in the wild for only a very short time. I haven't seen my mother or father in a coon's age and a coon's age is a very long time, I can tell you that! So, how in the world am I suppose to know what a baboon does or doesn't do, and why should I believe you anyway?"

"You can believe me because my mother is a teacher, and she's very smart." Priscilla answered in a somewhat defensive tone. "She knows all kinds of stuff, and she never lies, so anything she tells me is the truth. Now, as much as I would love to hear about your past history, I really can't afford the time because I need your help, and I need it right now!"

Her arm was growing numb, and the pain in her shoulder joint was almost unbearable. She reached with her other arm and felt the branch weaken some more.

The baboon could hear the fear in her voice. She was in a panic. He didn't blame her. She had actually behaved quite bravely up until this point especially when he considered that she was, after all, a girl, and that she was indeed dangling from a tree branch at least thirty feet off the ground.

The blue baboon was in a real dilemma.

"I really would like to try and save her," he said to himself, "but what if I can't do all those things she says I can do?"

He was filled with self-doubt.

"But what if you can?" an inner voice echoed in his confused mind.

He heard her branch crack. It was splitting away. Priscilla screamed.

She was falling.

5

The Blue Baboon

Priscilla couldn't tell if it was something she had said or if it was the baboon's own inner strength that somehow clicked in his brain at the last possible moment. He had grabbed her hand and swung her to his back, slick as a whistle. It was a ride she'd never forget.

With blue hair flowing and mouth wide open, the baboon had screamed all the way down the giant oak. Priscilla wondered if he didn't perhaps speak a second language for she had not understood many of the words yelled out by her blue-haired rescuer.

But it was the baboon's gifted tail that she would always remember. It gripped all the right branches all the way down the giant oak.

The landing had been a little rough, she had to

admit, and it was probably a miracle that she survived at all. But now as she lay in a heap at the base of the great tree, she looked up and saw how high she had gone. Priscilla shuddered at what could have been, and although she was covered with leaves and dirt, at least she wasn't hurt. She stood and brushed herself off then turned to the blue baboon. He was having the time of his life.

"Hey Kid, you gotta admit, now *that* was a fun ride!" the baboon proudly told her. He danced and pranced as he sang his own praises. "I did it. I did it. I really, really did it and what about this magnificent, one-of-a-kind tail of mine? Unbelievable, uh?"

He held his tail close to Priscilla's face then put it to his own lips. He kissed it several times before rubbing it softly against his cheek.

"It's unbelievable, all right," Priscilla mumbled under her breath. She watched the baboon carry on his own celebration and wondered, "Could this be the same creature that was terrified just a few short moments ago? How peculiar?"

"Hey, I just might be the greatest baboon of all time." He continued to boast as he twirled around

Priscilla. She couldn't help but roll her eyes. She checked her bonnet and was relieved to find it still tied tight and secure on her head.

"You know what Kid, I do believe that I qualify for a life-saving award," the baboon's eyes lit up at his own suggestion. "Wouldn't you agree, Missy?"

He didn't wait for her to answer but continued on with his bragging.

"As a matter of fact," he said, "I'm declaring myself a full-fledged hero as of right now. I am at your service madam." He bowed before Priscilla.

"Do you have a name?" The baboon asked her. "I really should know the name of the person I so bravely saved. Don't you think, huh?"

He was so proud of himself. It irritated Priscilla when she considered her near-fatal fall. She now turned and faced him. With gritted teeth the small girl slowly backed the blue baboon up to the great oak poking her finger repeatedly at is chest while talking in a controlled, firm tone.

"My name is Priscilla, Priscilla McDoodleNut-DoodleMcMae. I'm usually quite shy. I don't talk to strangers nor do I normally chitchat with stray baboons, but there is one thing I feel I must say to you."

The baboon was suddenly afraid of her. It was easy to see that she was quite irritated.

"And just what is it that you feel you need to say to me?" He asked in a weak voice.

"You could have gotten me killed, you crazy blue-haired monkey!" Priscilla screamed.

His eyes narrowed.

"She can't talk to me that way," he thought to himself. He quickly felt his confidence returning.

"Well, that's just rich, ain't it, oh Miss-High-and-Mighty Priscilla. There's gratitude for you," he said, shaking his head and throwing his arms up in the air. "No thank-you, no appreciation, no consideration for all I've done. Your little name-calling has cut me right here," he pointed to his heart, "and I can tell you, Miss Priscilla, it hurts. It hurts real bad!"

He faked a sob then turned away. He crossed his arms and waited.

"I have her now," he thought, fighting back a little smile. "She's feeling guilty. Imagine the nerve of her, calling me a crazy monkey when I was so brave and calm in such a dangerous situation."

He turned his head to see her reaction.

"He's so dramatic," she thought.

"I'm sorry," Priscilla said quietly. "Thank you for saving my life. How can I ever repay you?"

"Well, now that you bring it up, Kid," he said rubbing his chin. "How much money ya' got?"

"None," Priscilla answered shyly.

"Any stocks or bonds?" the baboon was all business now.

"No."

"Any property in your name?"

"No."

"Any time-shares?"

"No."

Sensing this could go on for awhile, Priscilla took a seat on an old log.

"Any rich old relatives near death who like you a lot and would consider leaving their fortunes to you?" the blue baboon continued.

"What a strange question," she thought, then answered, "no, no rich relatives."

"How about jewelry? Any diamonds, rubies or pearls?"

"No."

"How about fancy cars? Race cars, roadsters or convertibles?"

"No! No! And no!"

"Motorcycles, Harley-Davidsons, four wheelers?"

"No! No! And no!" She had no idea what he was talking about.

"Boats, fancy yachts, a condo, perhaps a second home on a tropical island with servants and . . . "

"No," Priscilla cut him off.

"A piggy bank?" he asked quietly, raising his hands and eyebrows.

"My piggy bank?" Priscilla was shocked. "You would actually ask for my piggy bank?"

"Well, okay, scratch the piggy bank," he said, a little embarrassed for having brought it up. "I guess I'm not quite that desperate for funds. Gee, Kid, if you don't mind me saying so, you're not really worth very much, are you?"

His words hurt, but the blue baboon did not seem to notice.

"I guess I never thought of myself as worthless

before," Priscilla said, with a hint of self-pity, "but, yes, if you're going to judge me by how much money I've got then I guess you're right. I'm not worth very much."

"Oh I didn't mean that comment the way it sounded, Kid. I was just referring to the monetary part of your life. I'm sure you're worth your weight in gold when it comes to the real person inside."

"It was an apology, well, sort of an apology," she thought, even if it didn't seem quite sincere.

He patted her head.

"There, feeling better now?" he asked.

"No, not really," her voice was quiet. "But there is one thing I can offer you."

"Save it," he said. "Consider the debt paid. After all, you did help me discover my tail. I never knew I had such an amazing talent."

"Oh yeah," Priscilla gulped, "I need to tell you something about that tail of yours."

"Yes. Go on." He looked at her with suspicion.

"Well, baboons don't normally have prehensile tails," she confessed.

"Pre-pre-hensile what?" the baboon was confused.

"You know," said Priscilla, "prehensile tails, tails that grip. Normally baboons do not swing from trees using their tails like other monkeys. I made that part up."

"You what?" he felt his blood pressure rising.

"Oh, members of your species are great tree climbers," Priscilla continued. "That part is true. You love to take naps in the branches or just chill out, but you spend most of your time on the ground."

His face was now beet red. "Why you little snit, you lied to me. I could have been killed!"

"Well, I had to think of something," she shouted back. "I was barely hanging on! It wasn't a full blown lie anyway," she felt the need to defend her actions. "Look at it this way. You discovered something about yourself today. You can swing from the trees using your tail. You are obviously one of the very fortunate few that must have inherited your prehensile, you know, your gripping tail from another primate, a primate on your family tree who has the same gift as you."

He said not a word. He only glared at her all the harder.

"Don't you get it?" Priscilla asked. "The DNA strand of molecules for a prehensile tail was passed onto you. Isn't that the most fascinating thing? Isn't nature wonderful? Isn't all science amazing?" Priscilla asked in awe.

"Oh yeah, it's wonderful and amazing and fascinating all right," he said, scowling at Priscilla while tapping his foot, his arms crossed in front of him. "I could have splattered all over the forest floor."

He shivered at the mere thought of it then continued his scolding.

"I could have broken my leg or my arm or my neck for cryin' out loud."

"Or your skull," Priscilla added with a smile. "Don't forget your skull."

"This is not funny!" The blue baboon was mad as she continued to grin.

"Oh, get a grip!" Priscilla fired back. "No one suffered any injury. We both landed on our feet, didn't we? Besides," she continued, "you owe me a debt of gratitude. Didn't I play a major role in your discovery? You probably would have never known about that tail of yours if I hadn't come along."

"She has a point," he thought. It was hard to admit, but she was right.

They stood staring at each other. Then, for no apparent reason, they both began to laugh, and their laughter was not the sound of a little chuckle or a couple of giggles. No, their laughter was from their guts, real belly laughs that shook their innards. And as they laughed the blue baboon recalled his amazing rescue of her. She was a brave girl and smart, too.

"Why, she's almost as brave and smart as I am," he thought.

"There is something I would like to give you," Priscilla said wiping away her tears of laughter.

"And what might that be, Miss Priscilla?" he asked while catching his breath.

She hesitated. "He has his faults, that's for sure. And he wasn't really all that brave. He liked to brag a lot, too. But underneath it all, she could tell he had a good heart and a feeling soul. Besides," she reminded herself, "no one's perfect."

Priscilla took a deep breath. The tone of her voice was most sincere as she addressed the blue baboon.

"I would like to offer you the gift of friend-ship," she said.

6

Oliver Matthew Molinka

The baboon went silent. The mood of the forest was suddenly very serious. Priscilla waited anxiously for his answer. She watched his nervous pacing and wondered what the baboon could possibly be thinking. She had expected a more spontaneous reaction to her offer.

"Well?" she questioned, looking up toward the blue baboon from the log she sat on. "What's your answer?"

He was clearly uncomfortable. Priscilla watched as he ran his hand several times through a blue tuft of hair that sprung out of control on the top of his head. At last he spoke.

"Look Priscilla, I don't mean to sound ungrateful but friendship involves trust, and I've learned not to trust anyone. Besides," he continued half-jokingly, "friendship doesn't pay well, if you know what I mean. It's not like you can deposit friendship in the bank."

She stared at him with an irritated look. She didn't like his teasing attitude right now.

"No, you can't take friendship to a bank," Priscilla's voice was stern and cold at the same time. "True friendship," she said, "is worth far more. And yes, true friendship involves trust, and trust builds character. And I'm sorry to disappoint you, but you can't deposit trust in some silly, old bank either!"

She swallowed hard, her eyes full of tears. She stood there looking at this odd-looking creature who for some strange reason, she thought, would make a great friend.

"Friendship," she said with a shaky voice, "is all I have to give."

She rose from the log and walked to the base of the huge oak. Her back now faced the baboon. She did not want to cry in front of him.

He stood there in the woods feeling miserable.

He was disgusted with himself. He had behaved badly. She had made a simple offer of friendship. It was all she wanted. He stood there embarrassed. He really was a crazy, blue-haired monkey.

"I'm sorry," the baboon said most sincerely. "If the offer is still open, I would consider it an honor to have you as a friend."

She turned and faced him, "You would?" Her voice was suddenly full of hope.

"Yes. Absolutely! You've got a friend in me," he answered. "Please forgive me."

"Of course," she said. "Friends forgive." Priscilla felt elated.

"By the way," she asked, "what's your real name?"

"My name is Oliver Matthew Molinka," the baboon answered with pride. "My mother would often times call me Ollie, and though it's been a long time since I've seen her or my father, I still remember the sound of their voices."

He smiled as he recalled his own sweet memories of them.

"Where are your parents, Ollie?" she asked in a timid, quiet voice, "and why haven't you seen them?"

She waited for him to answer but the blue baboon grew suddenly very quiet. He stared at the spiraling columns of the castle in the distance; his eyes were now filled with anger and frustration. Slowly he turned his head and faced her.

He wasn't sure why, but he trusted her. And so he began his story.

"It was a warm, summer day, years ago," the blue baboon recalled, "a perfect day for a stroll through the jungle. I remember playing in the tall grass while my mother and father looked on. They alerted me to stay within their view, but I did not heed their warnings. It wasn't long before I realized that I was lost.

"As luck would have it, Wynthor was out surveying the western part of the jungle on that very same day. He had declared large portions of the area his own and was in the process of staking out his claims when he discovered me. I tried to out run him, but he and his servants were faster.

"At first, he was quite taken with me. I was small and cute but most importantly, my hair was blue. Wynthor declared me his royal pet on the spot and the rest, as they say, is history. My mom and dad of course came looking for me. They fought hard to get me back, but his Royal Blue Majesty would not surrender what he called "his personal property." The protective instincts of both my mother and my father went wild. It took several servants to stop them from attacking old Wynthor. The blue-haired king immediately declared them insane and banished them to our sister moon forever. His order was carried out that very day. I haven't seen my parents since.

Priscilla could feel the blue baboon's sadness. Her own eyes filled with tears as Ollie finished his heart-breaking story. She could not imagine the pain of such an awful separation.

"I am so sorry, Ollie," Priscilla said with true sincerity. Then she added in a hopeful voice, "One day, I'm sure your family will have the opportunity to come home and reclaim you as their son."

"I hope you're right," Ollie replied, "but as much as I miss them, I'm actually glad they're not here. The moon is a dangerous place right now. Everyone is afraid, and fear can cloud the minds of leaders and citizens alike. We are forbidden to question, no one dares to ask *Why* and as a result our division grows wider everyday.

"My goal, at this stage of my life, is simple," said Ollie. "I hope to survive day by day without injury. This will not be easy to accomplish especially with Norman's old cat hanging around. That pompous, snobbish, big, know-it-all-kind of a feline loves to get others in trouble, and he's a bully, too."

"What's his name?" Priscilla was curious.

"The cat's name?"

"Yes, silly. The cat's name."

"Oh, he really doesn't have a name," Ollie said, "although, I did hear someone call him Rodney once. That's the one thing old Rodney and I have in common; no one knows or calls us by our given names."

"But that's so sad," Priscilla said.

Ollie shrugged his shoulders. "Yeah well, it's just the way things are. At least I have a roof over my head" he said, "and there are a few good things about living in a castle."

"Like what," asked Priscilla.

"Like sneaking around when nobody thinks

I'm there or hiding in places where no one would think to look, except maybe for Rodney." Ollie turned his nose up at the sound of the old cat's name. "Sometimes I pretend I'm a secret agent, listening and gathering all kinds of classified information and that's why I can tell you, Miss Priscilla, there's trouble brewing, big time trouble. That's for sure."

"My father works at the castle," Priscilla said with pride.

"Well then he can tell you" Ollie explained, "that living and working in a castle is not much fun, especially when forced to work with two old geezers like Norman and Wynthor."

Priscilla wondered as to what made up an old geezer. She had never heard the term before but decided not to interrupt Ollie. She would ask her father later.

"There are moments," the blue baboon continued, "when I feel like I may be stuck with old Wynthor and Norman for the rest of my life. Like you, I wait for better days, but in the meantime the castle is my home, no matter how much I dislike it.

"Believe me, it's not easy living with old King

Wynthor. He's a booger-eatin', toenail-chewin' butt-tootin' kind of a guy. I can't tell you how bad he stinks up the place with all that natural gas he expels. There are days when I swear he has a whole band tooting in his undershorts. That big-mouthed Norman is just as bad. They're both crazy, I tell you."

"My father thinks the kings are crazy, too, but I've never heard him say anything about a band playing in King Wynthor's undershorts," Priscilla giggled.

"Well, your father sounds like a good man, a man with insight, a man with intelligence, a man with good looks, just like me!" She was glad that Ollie's normal, fun-loving tone of voice had returned.

"I shall keep a sharp look-out for your dear father, introduce myself and then let him know what a fine daughter he has."

Priscilla shouted out a desperate, "*No!*"

"Why not?" Ollie was puzzled by her reaction.

"Just promise me you won't say anything to my father."

"She seems so intense," the baboon thought.

But aloud he said, "Yeah, okay, Kid. Don't have a stroke over it. Gee, you sure can get worked up over the littlest thing."

"It's not a little thing," she snapped back, "and you should respect the feelings of others."

"Hey, I'm respectful," he said firmly. "I did save your life. Remember?"

"Yes. You're right."

"Hey, I've got to get going. Wynthor will have my butt if he discovers I'm gone."

Ollie turned to Priscilla. He was surprised at how much he had enjoyed talking to her.

"Hey friend, let's meet back here this afternoon at one o'clock? That's when old Wynthor takes his four hour nap so I'm good to go at that time."

Priscilla hesitated. "I'll try to make it," she said, "but I can't promise. My parents are very protective of me."

"Why?" Ollie asked.

"Why what?"

"Why are your parents so protective of you?" he asked her while climbing the great oak.

"They have their reasons." Priscilla yelled so he could hear her.

"Okay! See ya' later, friend," Ollie shouted back.

"See ya' later, friend," she waved in his direction.

"He called me friend," Priscilla smiled, "Ollie called me friend."

She had started her walk back home when the tower chimed the eight o'clock hour. "Oh no," she thought.

She had lost track of time, and could now hear the kings in their usual, hateful morning debate.

"Blue is better than red!"

"No, reds are smarter!"

"Are not!

"Are too!'

"I hate your guts!"

"I hate yours more!"

"They're in rare form," thought Priscilla.

Her parents would probably wake. They would demand answers as to where she had been.

She started to run, picking up speed as she went down the hidden path, back toward the clearing.

7

Willa and Albert

Willa McDoodleNutDoodleMcMae awoke to the screaming voices of Kings Wynthor and Norman. It was the same old argument that somehow seemed louder than usual in this early morning hour.

She wondered, "Did someone turn up the volume on the speakers or have my ears developed a severe sensitivity to the kings' nonsense?

"Whatever the reason," she said to herself, "those two nuts in the castle are giving me a headache."

She shuffled to the kitchen in her pink bathrobe and bare feet. She needed a cup of strong, black coffee, and so she began her early morning brew. She then walked slowly to the bathroom where she stared at her reflection in the mirror, alone with her thoughts.

"Why do we allow selfish leaders like Wynthor and Norman to govern?" Willa questioned. "Will change ever come?"

She didn't know, but she was certain of one thing; fear and lack of courage would only prolong the madness.

She studied her reflection more closely. Her wild, curly, red hair was definitely out of control. "It looks like a bad hair day for me," she said out loud.

The high-pitched screaming of the two kings continued, but Willa was determined to drown them out. She would not allow Wynthor or Norman to ruin this perfect, summer morning, and so, she began to sing, not a nice, soft, romantic kind of a song; no, not Willa. She sang, instead, at the top of her lungs every rock n' roll tune she could think of. She sang all through her shower and while she styled her hair. She sang as she applied just enough make-up to highlight her green eyes and high cheek bones. She even sang while brushing her teeth.

Her singing continued as she now stood in front of her looking glass. "Yes," she sang triumphantly, "it's going to be a good hair day after all."

Willa was pleased with her reflection. She wore a short-sleeved white blouse neatly tucked in her denim jean skirt. Her pearl earrings, gold wedding ring and heart-shaped locket were the only jewelry items Willa owned. She kissed her locket before letting it dangle from a gold chain that hung around her neck. It contained two cherished photos: one of her daughter and one of her husband. She slipped into her brown sandals, took one last look in the mirror and began her brand new day.

Her first task of the morning, she decided, was to pull away the two pillows that covered her husband's head. There was no doubt that he had attempted to block out, not only the king's voices, but her singing as well.

"Wake up, you lazy bag of bones," she teased.

"I'll wake up if you quit singing," Albert replied.

She tousled his thick, blue hair.

"You don't like my singing?" she asked, pretending to look hurt.

"No, I don't like your singing," he said half-smiling, "at least not at eight o'clock in the morning."

He opened his eyes a little wider and then looked more closely at his attractive wife.

"Hey, don't you look sharp," he said. "Are you going somewhere today?" he asked.

"Well, yes, as a matter of fact I am," Willa informed him. "I plan to do some shopping at the castle square this afternoon."

She immediately saw the worried look on his face, and so she attempted to ease his mind.

"Albert, you know I would never leave Priscilla if I felt she wasn't safe. She's old enough to stay alone for short periods of time. She'll be fine here while I'm gone."

He could tell Willa's mind was made up.

"Besides," she continued, "today is a very special day, and there are some things that I absolutely must get from the market."

She wondered if he remembered.

"Like what things?" asked Albert.

"Oh, like some milk and eggs, a loaf of bread, some fruit for dinner." She rattled off her grocery list but kept silent about the very special anniversary gift she would purchase for her husband today. Willa had scrimped and saved for almost a year to buy an engraved, gold pocket watch. It would replace the cheap timepiece Albert now carried which ran either too slow or too fast or not at all. Her gift, she hoped, would make her husband's job a little easier especially since he worked for a king who was constantly screaming, "What time is it? What time is it?"

Albert was not interested in grocery lists or special gifts. His mind was elsewhere.

"That old Wynthor and Norman," Albert thought to himself. "What were those two clowns up to anyway?"

He had received a work order the day before commanding him and his fellow blue servants to work all night on what the kings called their *Special Project*. King Norman had sent the same order to his servants. No one knew, as of yet, what this *Special Project* entailed, but whatever it was, if Norman and Wynthor were involved, it meant trouble, big time trouble for them all.

Consequently, he did not like the idea of Priscilla alone in the cottage even for a short period of time, nor did he like the thought of Willa going to the castle square by herself. Albert knew firsthand of the increased tensions mounting between the red and the blue. These tensions greatly concerned him. The kings' hatred of one another and their individual quests for total and absolute power had reached a new level of intensity. These were dangerous times with dangerous ways of thinking, and Albert worried not only about his own family but for all those who called this moon their home. He could feel a great division growing like a terrible storm.

These concerns, he knew, made him over-protective at times. Normally he would take care of any necessary shopping or running of errands on his way home from work. On occasion, Willa would travel to the square if Albert happened to get home early enough. It was a rare thing to leave Priscilla alone.

Years ago on special days, Willa would take their daughter to the castle square. Each time Albert had disapproved of these outings, but each time he had given into the pleas of his daughter and wife.

"She'll have her bonnet on nice and snug," Willa would always promise.

At first the kids in the square only pointed fingers at Priscilla's bonnet, but soon they began to tease and call her names. Still, the young daughter begged to go, hopeful that one day others would accept her, but when several older kids actually attempted to pull her bonnet off, Albert and Willa both agreed; the risk was too great. Their daughter would need to live in isolation until things changed.

Priscilla had cried over their decision, yet, she understood her parent's fear of discovery.

"*Why* am I different?" she had asked her father. "*Why* do kids make fun of me? *Why* can't we play together as friends?"

And her *Why* questions would go on and on.

Albert had no answers then. He had no answers now.

The intolerance, the disrespect, the hurtful words and gestures continued. It was a terrible thing for his daughter to live in fear without friends her own age.

"Maybe," Albert thought, "my wife is right;

fear and lack of courage does indeed, allow the madness to go on."

The feel of Willa's hand in his brought his mind back to the present moment.

"I'll finish my shopping early and get back to Priscilla in record time," she said in her most caring voice.

Albert smiled. She had a way of melting his heart. He squeezed her hand.

"Just remember to stay away from all those single, red-haired lads when you go to the square. You're bound to get noticed looking as pretty as you do."

"Flattery will get you a cup of coffee and a hot breakfast," she said, and then closing the bedroom door behind her, she went to her kitchen to prepare a very special breakfast for a very special husband on this very special day.

8

The Day Begins

Albert could hear the kings' voices echoing off the hill from the blaring loudspeakers.

"Another long day at the castle," he groaned.

He pulled the pillow back over his head. He felt tired, and yet his day was just beginning. He thought about staying home but was obligated to his responsibilities.

He was Wynthor's senior servant and therefore a man of importance. His presence at the castle was needed. So he rose from their bed and readied himself for a very long day.

He could hear Willa complaining to herself in the kitchen. She was especially annoyed with the kings today. Albert didn't blame her. He would need to work late tonight and that was disappointing for he knew she had planned something very special.

Willa was normally a fun-loving person with a positive attitude and even when worry and isolation seemed too much to bear, she somehow always found a reason to smile.

"One day things will change and all our *Whys* will have answers," Albert had repeatedly told her.

"But, when?" Willa wondered. Her mind was so intent on the answer to her question that she failed to notice the empty swing hanging motionless from the tree.

"Those two old geezers," Willa complained under her breath as Albert entered the kitchen.

His blue hair was styled neatly, and in spite of his blue jacket, his blue-laced shirt, his blue-striped socks and blue leather shoes, Albert looked quite handsome. She knew her husband disliked his job intensely and his work clothes even more.

"I look like a blue-haired clown," he would often say.

But at least Albert had a place of employment, and though he didn't get paid all that much, his wages did put food on the table.

He poured himself a cup of coffee then glanced out the window. He could see Priscilla in her usual spot gently swaying on her swing.

"Make sure her bonnet is on extra tight when you leave for the square today," Albert ordered. "I want her hair covered at all times. Someone might mistakenly come to the door."

"But Albert," Willa said, "she hates that bonnet, and you did tell her she could go without it indoors."

"Not if she's alone," Albert was firm.

The situation frustrated Willa. "I am half-tempted to march right into that castle myself and give old Norman and Wynthor a piece of my mind," she said to he husband.

Albert stepped back and sipped his coffee. He smiled to himself as he observed his wife. She was a feisty one. He remembered their very first meeting. She had been a teacher, and he a messenger for King Wynthor. He recalled delivering a signed order that commanded every moon teacher to separate all children into groups according to their color of hair: red or blue. The moon kids, according to the order, could no longer sit or play or learn together. It was a ridiculous rule and one that Willa refused to obey.

Albert had continued to deliver repeated written orders, but with each message Willa became more determined to resist. She began to publicly challenge what she called an idiotic law and was even heard using the *Why* word at times. Albert understood her frustration and agreed with her thinking, but he secretly worried about her future for the kings would never tolerate what they called a rebellious attitude.

It wasn't long before Albert's concern grew into heartfelt caring, but the kings' law of separation pertained not only to the moon children but to all adults as well. It was, of course, a senseless law but a law all the same: no red-haired man or woman was allowed to mingle either publicly or privately with a blue-haired person and vice versa. Any serious or romantic relationship was strictly forbidden.

And so Albert and Willa began meeting secretly. He loved her red hair and the way she laughed and what she stood for. She in turn loved his gentle spirit and the way he worried and cared for others. Then came that awful day when she was removed from her classroom. She was banned from all moon schools forever. No longer could she teach, and if she dared to disobey, she would face certain banishment. The thought of Willa living thousands and thousands of miles away was too much for Albert to bear. He vowed to love and protect her all the days of his life.

"She had made a beautiful bride," he now recalled. He remembered her moonlit face, their spoken vows and the warmth of her hand. "Twelve years ago today," he thought.

Though secretly married, they had made a good life together. Albert's little cottage, where he had once lived alone, became their home together. They were happy and yet lack of freedom had created stress and strain for each of them.

Albert often relied on Willa's strength of character. "She's a strong woman," he thought, "but even the strong have their limits." He was equally concerned about his daughter, Priscilla, who at times was very much like her mother. "No telling what could happen," he thought, "if their two strong spirits were ever set loose together."

Willa continued to sputter as she flipped pancakes and scrambled the eggs. The smell of bacon found its way to Priscilla on the swing. She was starving. It certainly had been an eventful morning, and all the activity had made her hungry.

She was grateful for the added minutes on the swing. The extra time had given her a chance to catch her breath after running the entire way home. Had she made it back in time? She wasn't sure. At least she hadn't found her parents desperately searching for her. That was a good sign.

"So far, so good," thought Priscilla.

Albert called to his daughter. "Come and get it, hon'. Breakfast is served."

She breathed a sigh of relief. She had made it. She could tell by her father's tone of voice.

She jumped from the swing and waved to her father. "I'm coming," Priscilla called back.

She started to run. Her bonnet loosened. It slipped down her back with the ties still around her neck. She ran across the clearing, her purple hair flowing freely in the wind.

9

Red and Blue Make Purple

Priscilla could tell her father was upset the second she entered the cottage.

"How many times have I told you not to take your bonnet off until you are in the house?" Albert scolded.

"I'm sorry, Dad" she said relieved. "It just loosened up on me."

"I don't mean to get upset with you, Priscilla but you must listen and then do as I say. It's for your own good."

She threw her arms around him, "Yes, Dad," she promised.

Breakfast never tasted quite so good. She was

still a little shaky when she remembered her near fall.

"Perhaps one day down the road," Priscilla thought, "I will share my rescue story with them but not today."

"The kings are in rare form this morning, don't you think?" Albert said, shaking his head. "Thank goodness the loudspeakers go off at 9:00 a.m. Our ears can rest then."

"I refuse to discuss those two old geezers," Willa said. She was still mad at the kings for having spoiled her plans for the evening.

Priscilla caught her father's frown.

"What's a geezer?" she asked. It was the second time today that she had heard that term.

"It's an old fart," Willa quickly responded.

"Willa!" Albert was about to scold when Priscilla interjected.

"It's okay, Dad," she said matter-of-factly. "I already know that Wynthor and Norman are a couple of old geezers with a major, internal, gas problem. I'll bet they toot most of the day away creating all kinds of weird sounds, like a band playing in their undershorts. I'm sure they can really stink up a place."

Albert and Willa both choked on their coffee for a second or two, their eyes opening wide at what their daughter had just said.

"Priscilla, that is not appropriate talk at the table or any other place for that matter," her father said trying to keep a stern tone.

Priscilla looked at her mother who was now hiding her face in her napkin. She was having a good laugh, the kind of laugh that makes a belly shake.

"Listen to your father," Willa managed to say.

Priscilla giggled. She thought of Ollie and King Wynthor's undershorts and then laughed all the harder.

Albert pretended to scold them both. "This is not funny," he said.

"Oh, yes it is," Willa said with tears running down her face. "It's about the funniest thing I've ever heard."

Albert, unable to contain himself any longer, threw his head back and laughed till his side ached.

"Little do they know," he thought, "that the

kings do indeed have a problem with gas. What Priscilla had said was true."

"Enough. Enough," he finally ordered. "My stomach hurts. I need to leave for work soon so let's get control of ourselves and finish this delicious breakfast before it gets cold."

Willa and Priscilla nodded in agreement as they let out a couple of final giggles. They ate in silence for a few moments before Albert spoke again.

"How is it," he said playfully, "that I am sitting here with the two most beautiful ladies in all the land?"

"I guess some guys have all the luck, right Priscilla?" Willa said, winking at her daughter.

"Have I ever told you," Albert directed his next question to Priscilla, "that purple is my favorite color?"

"Only every day, Dad."

Priscilla glanced at her mother and father as they sat eating. "They make a handsome couple," she thought.

Most importantly, she liked their way of thinking. They were funny and loving even when they teased one another. Most importantly, they respected each other in a very cool way. She especially liked the way her father looked at her mother. It made her feel safe.

"Do you know why today is a special day?" Albert asked Priscilla while smiling at his wife.

Willa looked toward her husband. "I thought maybe you had forgotten."

"Not a chance," Albert said shaking his head.

"Well, what day is it?" asked Priscilla. "I know it's not my birthday."

"No," said Albert, "it's not your birthday. It's Reverend Thomas T. Tooker Day."

10

Reverend Thomas T. Tooker and the Sister Moon

Priscilla noticed her mother now smiling a different kind of smile. Her flushed cheeks made her eyes even more beautiful.

"I've never heard of Reverend Thomas T. Tooker before," said Priscilla. "Who is he?"

Sensing a tale regarding this mysterious character was about to begin, Priscilla did what she always did when her father started to share his own recollections of different people and events; she sat on his lap.

Willa observed the two of them. They were bonded in a special way.

She remembered the night Priscilla was born. Willa's own fear of discovery had forced her and her husband to bring their new daughter into the world alone.

She remembered Albert's pride when he announced, "It's a girl!" Never had she felt such a rare and overwhelming love. It was a mother's love, and when she touched the face of her child, Willa knew that her daughter was destined to fulfill some meaningful purpose. That same sense of purpose was as strong today as it had been then.

Now, as she watched Priscilla with her father, she suddenly was afraid for she, like Albert, felt a great storm looming on the horizon. Their futures held many unknowns. Yet she was confident as well. The three of them could face anything so long as they were together, and with that thought in mind she decided to put aside her worries for the moment and listen to the story of Reverend Thomas T. Tooker.

"Reverend Thomas T. Tooker was a very special person who once lived on our moon." Albert began. "He secretly married your mother and me on this very date twelve years ago and I, for one, am forever grateful to him for providing us with such an important service."

"Me, too," giggled Priscilla.

Albert caught Willa's eye and smiled.

"Did Reverend Tooker get into trouble when he married you and mom?" asked Priscilla, for she knew that reds were not allowed to mix with the blues.

"No." Albert answered. "He kept our marriage a secret, but he did one thing that no one else had ever done before. He dared to ask *Why?*

"I remember the day well," Albert recalled. "Thomas had stood in the castle square, straight and tall. He had spoken on more than one occasion against the unfair practices of the kings and because he spoke his mind, Norman and Wynthor called a special meeting. Those who were present, including myself, listened to the false accusations made against Thomas by each king."

Priscilla noticed her father's sad, faraway look as he went on with his story.

"It was terribly unjust," Albert continued. "Both kings had hearts of stone. I saw the hate in their eyes. Their screaming and yelling went on for what seemed like hours. Then, at last, it was

Reverend Tooker's turn to speak. There were many citizens present. We all watched as Thomas calmly stood before their royal majesties. If he was afraid, he didn't show it. He was ready to challenge both Wynthor and Norman even if it meant standing alone.

"But when Thomas went to speak, the kings would not listen. They had closed not only their ears but their minds as well. So Reverend Tooker, in his wisdom, decided to question their ridiculous laws. He looked straight into the cold eyes of each king and in front of everyone asked them a series of questions, '*Why* do you divide us? *Why* do you rule with contempt in your hearts, and *Why* can't we all live in peace where justice is served and all citizens are treated with respect? For no one person is more important than the other including your majesties?'

"The kings, of course, had no answers to these questions, and so they reacted by throwing a terrible fit. They pounded the table. They stomped on the floor. They held their breaths till their faces almost exploded. They screamed and they hollered

64

and shook a tight fist. It was the worst two temper tantrums anyone had ever seen.

"The kings banished Reverend Tooker that very day."

"But what did everyone else do?" Priscilla's innocent question tugged at Albert's conscience.

"We did nothing," Albert answered quietly. "I, along with everyone else who was present, just stood there and did nothing."

The cottage fell silent. Willa knew her husband often regretted his silence that day, but he had been torn between his family responsibilities and his duty as a citizen.

"Reverend Tooker knew how bad I felt," Albert told Priscilla. "I remember looking into his eyes. He was my dear friend, and I had let him down or so I thought. He had every right to feel disappointed and abandoned, but instead Thomas left that day with no ill-feeing toward anyone. His last words to me before his forced departure were filled with understanding.

"He simply whispered, 'Sometimes there is no right or wrong answer. Sometimes there is only the burden of making a difficult choice.'"

Priscilla sat silent for a few moments. She could see her father's pain.

"Where is Reverend Tooker now?" she asked.

"He was sent to our sister moon."

"Can you tell me more about our sister moon?" asked Priscilla.

"It's a moon very much like our own," Albert told her. "There are many moons in our galaxy, but our individual sister moon is special because of its unique reflective glow."

"I don't think I've ever seen it." Priscilla said.

"Oh, it happens on a very rare occurrence." Albert told his wide-eyed daughter. "It becomes visible only if the northern sky is perfectly clear and the orbit of our sister moon spins at the exact same speed as our home moon. When that happens a gravitational pull allows beams of light to travel across an invisible line. Those beams reflect back a beautiful colored glow that can illuminate the deepest, darkest part of any forest, and once you've seen it, there's no mistaking from where it came."

"I've seen this rare glow only once," said Albert, his voice now soft and mysterious. "It not only lit the darkness in a strange but beautiful way, it also gave me reason to hope that change will come and that one day Reverend Thomas T. Tooker and all those like him will return to live in peaceful coexistence with all those who call this moon their home."

Priscilla listened with great interest. She wanted to hear more about Reverend Tooker and the sister moon, but she knew her father must be on his way.

Albert checked his watch. He wasn't quite sure of the time but knew he must depart.

He kissed his daughter's cheek.

He embraced his wife.

"Happy Anniversary," he whispered.

"Happy Anniversary," Willa replied softly.

"Wear your bonnet today," Albert pointed his finger at Priscilla.

"I will," she promised.

And then he was out the door. The air was quiet. The kings' voices were no longer heard.

"I can hear the birds again," Albert called.

Priscilla stood by Willa at the cottage window. Together they watched her father walk straight and tall across the clearing. He turned one last time to wave good bye before stepping into the forest to the hidden path that would take him to the castle.

Part Two

And they argued for hours. They argued all night.

They argued who's wiser. They argued who's right.

They pounded the table. They stomped on the floor.

They made such a racket then argued some more.

But those who were present, they heard not a word

For they were all sleeping. Not one of them stirred

Except for Priscilla and Wynthor's baboon

Who feared for all people who lived on their moon.

11

The Castle Square

Albert stood observing the crowd from the castle entrance. He was surprised at the number of citizens entering the square so early in the morning. Most were simple travelers eager to see what bargains they might find. Others were farmers and peasants who had come long distances pulling carts filled with homemade breads, jams and fresh picked fruits and vegetables.

There were even a few visitors who hauled wagons filled with cut flowers of every variety. These early morning blooms represented every color of the rainbow, each with their own unique fragrance. The smell of roses, lilacs and azaleas, just to name a few, filled the air with a luring scent.

The square was an important place for all those who resided on the moon. It was the heart of the kingdom where citizens gathered for meetings and visited with friends and neighbors.

It was also a place where red and blue-haired merchants proudly displayed their goods in many quaint, little shops. At one time both red and blue shopkeepers had mingled together setting up their wares on both sides of the square with no regard for a person's color of hair. Shoppers did the same, crossing from side to side to inspect the goods of all vendors. Their interactions with sellers had normally created an inviting atmosphere but not today.

Instead, feelings of growing distrust and superiority created an increasing dislike between red and blue-haired citizens. They pointed fingers and made serious accusations against one another. Their insulting remarks were mean and hurtful and always directed to those whose hair color was different than their own. Places of business were now, per order of the kings, arranged in the same way as the castle: shop owners with red hair to the east and those with blue to the west. Farmers and peasants selling their goods followed suit. It was a crazy way of thinking, and it caused Albert to worry about Willa's planned visit to the market place today.

He knew his wife would wear a smile and speak to everyone, but this crowd would turn their noses up at anyone who offered a warm greeting. This negative reaction to Willa's friendly approach would puzzle her. She might even challenge someone with that feisty spirit of hers if they were rude or insulting.

"I will need to keep a close lookout," Albert thought to himself. Finding Willa in such a crowd might prove to be difficult, but then he smiled. He could spot that redhead a mile away.

In the meantime there was nothing to do except wait, and while he waited Albert studied the castle more closely. Its drab, gray, stone walls seemed to reflect the moon's escalating turmoil. Two large stone pillars reaching high in the sky, marked dividing lines for the castle grounds. A single clock tower stood between the pillars. This tower, sadly, was the only thing shared by the two stubborn kings.

At the top of the pillar just east of the clock, there waved a red flag, while the pillar to the west waved blue. But the main focus of the square was the royal platform which jutted out like a giant stage into an open area. It stood approximately six feet above the ground. The platform held two thrones, one trimmed with red rubies and one with blue sapphires. Each throne was placed directly in line with its coordinating flag. Open staircases, one red and one blue, extended out from the royal platform and down to the ground level. These stairs were originally constructed so that common citizens could approach their leaders to discuss important issues. The kings deemed the stairs privileged. And since no one was considered "worthy" or "royal" enough to even approach the thrones, the stairs were of no use, and their majesties remained unchallenged.

From where he stood, Albert could see dark doorways leading to huge royal kitchens and several massive dining and meeting rooms, all of which were cold and uninviting. The dimly lit hallways smelled of mold and mildew, which contributed to the already dismal atmosphere. There was no color, no music, no art or theater, no good morning greetings and worst of all, there was no joy or laughter.

Albert continued to keep a watchful eye while performing his daily duties. These duties included a daily inspection of the castle's four main floors. Here on the first floor, Albert wasted no time. He checked on all things that were deemed valuable by order of the kings. These included framed, hand-painted portraits of their royal majesties. The portraits depicted each king showing off their jeweled crowns, their velvet coats and their hair, always their hair piled high and haughty on top of their heads.

Albert next entered an open stairwell which led him to the second floor. Chambermaids followed with their mops and buckets. Together they opened the large wood door that led to Wynthor and Norman's private quarters. The maids, sensing Albert's need to hurry, mopped the floors, made up the royal beds and tidied up the kings' messy rooms in record time. Meanwhile Albert inspected yet more matted picture frames hanging on cold, second floor walls.

Here, enlarged photos portrayed Wynthor and Norman as mighty body builders. They posed in tight red and blue bathing suits while flexing their puny muscles, each claiming to have greater physical strength. The kings looked so ridiculous that Albert laughed in spite of himself.

But that laughter was short-lived for there was nothing funny about the dreaded third and fourth floors. These two areas were originally meant to serve as entertainment rooms for invited guests but since no one was ever invited, the third and fourth levels were left to the spiders, bats and scurrying rats to destroy.

As Albert ascended the stairs, eerie sounds echoing throughout the dungeon-like hallway made him nervous. He decided to perform what he called a "quick look inspection." He simply peeked in each room, secured the doors and called it good.

His inspection duty now complete, it was time for the royal procession to begin. Albert dutifully took his place in line on the platform and as he did so, he noticed two large delivery carts unloading gallons and gallons of paint along with many heavy-duty brushes.

"Could this have something to do with the kings' *Special Project*," he wondered.

The sight left Albert with an uneasy feeling. For the kings were capable of just about anything.

"Let's get this show on the road," snapped Wynthor.

"Oh, shut up," yelled Norman.

"No! You shut up," screamed Wynthor. "What time is it anyway?" he barked, not bothering to check the clock tower behind him.

"I say again, what time is it?" He directed his anger now toward his tall, blue-haired servant.

Albert checked his timepiece. It had stopped again. He closed it quickly.

"We're right on time, Your Majesty."

"Are you sure?" The blue-haired king asked with suspicion.

"Quite sure, Your Majesty," replied Albert.

Both kings grunted as they performed one final inspection of their attendants. Everyone was accounted for including the royal pets who always brought up the rear of the royal line. They waited now in single file for the sound of trumpets which would signal the procession of kings and servants to the royal platform.

There, the daily duties of the kings would begin. Every morning was the same. An agenda was always placed in the hands of each king. It provided a list of concerns as outlined by the moon's citizens. But Norman and Wynthor were far too busy promoting their own self images to ever take notice. They had little or no time to address what they called "trivial nonsense" from "common folk."

"The time, the time!" screamed Wynthor again.

"If you don't shut that trap of yours," Norman threatened, "then I will shut it for you!" The kings were now in each others faces.

"Oh yeah."

"Yeah!"

"Oh yeah!

"Yeah!"

Albert motioned to the royal trumpeters. The sound from their instruments muted the kings' voices, and the procession began.

"There's big time trouble brewing," Albert thought to himself. He could feel it in his bones and in the eyes of the blue baboon who for some odd reason kept staring at him. Could it be that this creature felt a danger as well and what about all of those paint cans? What did it all mean?

Soon, very soon, he would have the answers to his questions.

12

King Norman

King Norman had his own unique look. He had a very round head with a very large mouth that rarely stopped giving orders. The shape of his head matched the shape of his belly except his belly was much larger and much rounder. He had very skinny arms and legs and his I'm-much-smarter-than-you attitude projected from every part of him.

He constantly turned his nose up at all blue-haired citizens, but his hatred of Wynthor was especially intense. Norman believed that redheads possessed a far superior brain then that of blue-haired people. He had no scientific evidence to prove such a claim, but he believed it anyway. His crazy thinking was based on ignorance and an ill-fed passion that was rooted in his obsession for power. The outward symbol of that power, he thought, was represented in his thick, red hair.

Norman sat smug on his red, ruby chair. "You fool," yelled Norman as he rudely grabbed the mirror from his servant to examine his hair. "You need to get my curls much higher."

At this, Norman took a large tube of styling gel and began squeezing gobs and gobs of the sticky, gooey stuff onto the top of his own head.

"Like this! Like this!" Norman screamed as he demonstrated what he called "the art of curl making."

The red and blue-haired attendants glanced at each other. They tried not to laugh at the antics of the red-haired king, but it was difficult. The gel, they could see, was so thick that it looked like clear snot dripping from his hair onto his nose and then into his very large mouth which was always open. Norman, however, was so into his hair that he never noticed his gooey, messed up face. He gazed into his mirror with haughty pride and self-admiration ready now to show off his red curls.

But when Norman stood for all to see, he accidentally stepped on the royal cat's tail. The cat's name was Rodney, and he had stared at Ollie the entire morning with an evil grin upon his face. It was the kind of grin that seemed to have a message, a message that made Ollie nervous because he knew first hand of Rodney's ability to make life miserable. So when Rodney screeched out in pain, Ollie couldn't help but smile with smug satisfaction.

But as the royal cat's tail remained under King Norman's heavy foot, it was easy to see that Rodney was in severe pain. Ollie watched in anger at Norman's abusive treatment. When the red-haired king was finished with his tirade, he lifted his foot with no apology. The royal cat simply crawled back to his position next to Norman's feet while his royal highness continued on with his ridiculous commands.

"Start my pedicure," screamed Norman. One of his servants immediately came running with a foot bath in hand, while another removed King Norman's shoes and socks.

"You fool! The water's too cold!" barked Norman after testing it with the tips of his toes. "Can't you do anything right?" he shrieked while kicking and splashing water into the eyes of those around him including Wynthor.

"Quit your splashing and your yelling," ordered the blue-haired king, "or you'll be sorry!"

"Oh yeah," Norman responded. "I'm not afraid of you."

"I'm warning you," Wynthor's voice was threatening.

"Is this better, Your Majesty?" the red-haired servant politely asked, while pouring warmer water into Norman's foot bath.

"Is what better?" the old king snapped, moving onto his next command.

"Where is my royal chef?"

The royal, red chef came forward.

"Yes, Your Majesty. What is your wish?"

"I'm hungry. Can't you hear my stomach growling? Feed me some red grapes."

"Yes, Your Majesty, and what can I prepare for your royal dinner this evening?" he asked, dropping grapes into Norman's big mouth.

"Hmmm, let me think," Norman said, drumming his fingers. "How about red lobster tails and red shrimp cocktail? Make sure it's a fresh catch of the day for if it's not, you will receive a royal smack. My taste buds are so refined that I can tell a day old fish from a fresh one, so beware!"

"You will of course present my dinner on my red china. You are to serve my finest red wine in my crystal red goblet. And to start off my royal dinner, I would like a very large red bowl of bean soup."

There were immediate groans from both sides of the platform, for each servant knew the price for bean soup; the whole castle would smell from here to high heaven and the reeking, royal, inner gases that Norman was sure to expel would make for a long night, indeed.

Norman turned and gazed with a daring look at all those groaning.

"Enough," Norman ordered while pointing his finger at both the red and blue servants. "Any more complaining and I will have you all flogged."

"Oh, hogwash," said King Wynthor while passing gas. "I'll flog my own servants."

The morning dragged on with Norman constantly yelling orders.

"Get me a drink! Fan me faster! Comb my hair! File my nails! Massage my feet! No, not that way, you fools! Idiots! I'm surrounded by idiots!"

Wynthor couldn't take the screaming anymore. He stepped out of his own foot bath, and when Norman looked away, the blue-haired king dumped his own royal toe-jam, foot water onto Norman's royal head.

13

King Wynthor

Norman stood rigid on the royal platform, his back toward Wynthor who was now snickering at the sight of the red king's drenched hair.

Many onlookers gasped at the events unfolding but others had all they could do to hold back their laughter.

"I'll get you for this," Norman said through gritted teeth.

"Oh, I'm really scared," mocked Wynthor.

"You should be scared, you stupid, blue-haired ox. Do you remember the time I shaved your ugly moustache off in your sleep or the time I dyed those weird eyebrows of yours a bright red?" Norman smiled as he recalled the mean memories. "Watch your back you wretched fool," Norman warned with a threatening voice, "because I intend to make you pay big time for dumping your gross, toe-jam water onto my royal head."

Wynthor's face turned crimson as he recalled the tricks Norman had played on him in the past.

"I'm not afraid of you," laughed the blue-haired king. But it was a nervous kind of laugh. He coped with that nervousness in the only way he knew how; he began screaming orders at his own servants.

"What time is it?"

Albert opened his broken pocket watch again.

"It's time for lunch, Your Majesty."

"Well then, where's my royal chef?" demanded Wynthor.

"I'm here, Your Majesty," the blue-haired chef came forward. "What is your wish?"

"Skip lunch," he yelled. "Norman just killed my appetite."

The red-haired king sat smirking on his throne while his servants filed his nails and tended his hair. He was thoroughly enjoying Wynthor's apparent discomfort.

"And what shall I serve you this evening?" the blue-haired chef asked in his most polite way.

"I would like fresh-caught blue gills for my

main course," Wynthor answered. "Serve them up with blue cheese, blueberry muffins, blueberry cheesecake and blue moon ice cream. I will expect the finest wine served out of a blue bottle into my blue goblet, and oh yes, make sure you start the evening meal with a big, blue bowl of bean soup."

The servants once again caught each other's eyes for they knew, based on past experiences, that once those beans started passing through the kings' royal digestive tracts, there was no stopping the power from within.

The servant's only hope for relief of the stench was to bring their Super-Duper-Nose-Closers. These little devices made out of clothespins and designed by the blue baboon were quite effective. They helped to block the smell considerably. Hopefully, Mother Nature would cooperate and send a nice breeze to help clear the air tonight, making the long hours more tolerable.

His meal orders now given, Wynthor began barking other commands, and though he'd never admit it, his orders were every bit as ridiculous as Norman's.

"No, no, no!" Wynthor yelled while pulling his

right foot up to his face, "I want my toenails shorter than that."

Everyone watched as the crazy king started chewing on his big toe. He chewed and gnawed till the thick, hardened nail was finally free. Then spitting it out, he stuck his foot in his servant's face and said, "Like this. Now get it right or you will receive a royal smack. Is that understood?"

"Yes, Your Majesty."

"I'd like to royal smack him," Ollie thought.

On the outside, the blue-haired king looked much different than his rival, Norman. Wynthor was skinny with a long, narrow face. He had big, thick, bushy eyebrows that extended off his stern-looking forehead and a handlebar moustache that hid his mean upper lip. He always tried to make himself look good by kneeling with his hands prayerfully folded, but his heart was no different than Norman's.

Both kings were hardened with no love or sense of caring for anyone except themselves. They had no idea how to govern in a fair and just manner, and like most leaders who attempt to rule without humility or compassionate wisdom, their respective kingdoms were now in grave danger, for hate was slowly poisoning the minds and the hearts of those who lived there.

The blue-haired king kept mumbling under his breath. His irritation with Norman soon gave way to intense anger, and when his anger turned to rage, everyone knew who would bare the brunt of Wynthor's wrath.

The blue-haired king grabbed Ollie's soft, blue hair with his rough hands. The scared, little baboon, with clenched teeth, waited now on Wynthor's lap, for he had been through this before.

"That Norman makes me so mad." Wynthor directed his comments to the baboon alone. "I'm the one with the smarter brain. I know everything about everything." He shook the baboon's shoulders.

"Why don't others understand me? I'm practically a saint," the blue-haired king shouted at the baboon while lifting him high in the air.

"*Why* must everyone make life so difficult? "Tell me *Why!*" screeched the old king.

He now had Ollie by the throat, and he shook him till it looked as if the pet baboon's eyes might pop out of his head.

"Excuse me," Ollie squeaked, "but isn't it against the law to ask *Why?*"

"How dare you question me?" Wynthor's anger grew even more intense. "Don't you know that I am above the law? Don't you know that I can say and do as I please? Don't you know anything?"

Ollie's face was now turning a dark blue as he dangled in midair with Wynthor's hand around his neck.

"Ouch!" screeched Wynthor as he dropped Ollie back to the platform floor. "Who pulled my hair?"

"A thousand pardons, Your Majesty," said Albert. "It was an accident. You see, you had a rather large snarl in your gorgeous, blue hair, and I must have accidentally pulled it."

Albert winked at the baboon.

"Well, see that you're more careful next time." Wynthor warned. "I'm allergic to pain, you know. It makes me crazy."

"Crazy-er," the baboon whispered under his breath.

"What did you say?" The king grabbed the baboon again.

"Amazing," Ollie choked out the word, "I said you were amazing."

Wynthor tossed the blue royal pet to the side. He was tired of morning chores and pet baboons and inferior redheads.

"It's time for my royal nap," declared Wynthor.

"It's time for my royal nap," stated Norman.

"You're such a copycat," Wynthor sneered with disgust.

"No! You are!" yelled Norman.

With that both kings went up the stairwell to the second floor, down their separate hallways and into their royal chambers, tooting all the way. Together they left a trail of stinky air that would only intensify overnight. But for now, at least, both kings were gone, and Ollie was glad for that.

He sat and rubbed his sore neck for a minute or two and then watched as the senior, blue-haired servant bent down to pick up a wadded agenda. Ollie could see the worry in Albert's face as he read the wrinkled paper. The small baboon, not wanting to leave the platform before expressing his gratitude, scampered to where Albert stood.

"Uh, excuse me, Sir," the baboon's voice was

respectfully shy, "but I wanted to thank you for pulling King Wynthor's hair at just the right moment."

Albert smiled, and when he smiled the blue baboon knew that this man was indeed Priscilla's father.

"You're welcome," replied the tall, gentle, blue servant. He extended his hand for Ollie to shake, and suddenly it occurred to the blue baboon that he had just made a second friend.

The thought comforted him because he had a strange inner feeling that he was going to need all the friends he could get.

14

Albert's Gift

The box was wrapped in pink, shiny paper with a white satin bow. It layed upon her pillow with a note that read:

> *To my beautiful red-haired lady,*
> *One Day . . .*
> *With love, Albert*

She had gone into the bedroom to dust, never expecting an anniversary surprise. She called to Priscilla, who lounged on the sofa, pretending to read her science book. The young daughter entered her mother's bedroom and knew immediately the reason for her calling.

"Oh, Mom!" said Priscilla. "Dad must have placed it there before leaving for work."

Priscilla took the small gift in her own hands and gave it a gentle shake.

"What do you think it is?" she asked her mother.

"I have no idea," replied Willa. "Should I open it now or wait till your father comes home?"

"Oh, open it now, Mom. Please." Priscilla begged. "Dad would never have left it here if he didn't want you to have it. Besides, he's gone until tomorrow, and I don't think I could wait that long."

"Me either," Willa smiled at her daughter's enthusiasm.

Priscilla placed the wrapped gift in her mother's hands. Slowly, Willa removed the satin bow and pink paper exposing a burgundy, velvet box. She opened it and then lifted the delicate hair comb for Priscilla to see. Priscilla's eyes, so much like her mother's, stared in awe.

"Oh, Mom," Priscilla spoke in a whisper. "It's beautiful."

The jeweled comb glittered in the light of the day. It was made of gold with red and blue stones attached. These stones surrounded a large purple gem. The effect was stunning, the meaning clear.

Priscilla smiled. She watched as her mother secured the decorative comb in her hair. The gems reflected and sparkled with every turn of her head.

"You look beautiful, Mom." Priscilla said.

"Willa stared at her own reflection in the mirror. The comb was a gift she would forever cherish. It was perfect.

The clock on the mantel chimed the hour. Taken in by the moment, Priscilla had forgotten the time.

"Ollie," she thought. She had to act quickly.

"Mom, let me finish the dusting," Priscilla offered. "You can run your errands and shop at the castle square just like you planned. I know how anxious you are to pick up Dad's gift."

"Well," Willa said with some doubt in her voice, "are you sure you can manage?"

She thought of Albert's concerns and now wondered if she should leave Priscilla alone.

"Mom, I'm old enough to care for myself," the confident young daughter responded a little impatiently. "Besides," she continued, "a girl needs a little time alone now and then. You said so yourself."

"Well, you've got me there. I believe I did say

those very words," Willa replied. "All right then, I suppose this is a good time to go, and you're right, I am very anxious to pick up your father's gift."

Priscilla grabbed her mother's purse and handed it to her.

Willa paused and looked at her daughter a little more intently.

"Say," she said. "You seem rather anxious to get me out of here. What have you got cooking in that purple-haired head of yours?"

Her mother was always very perceptive. She never missed a wayward look or a subtle change in the tone of a voice. It seemed, at times, as if Willa could read minds, especially the mind of her daughter.

"I don't know what you're talking about," Priscilla sounded fairly convincing. "Please, don't worry, Mom. Go and enjoy yourself. After all you need to show off your beautiful, new hair comb."

Willa reached for her hair and touched her gift again. She smiled at her daughter. "Yes, it might be fun to strut my stuff," she said jokingly, "but, before I go, let's review a few rules.

"Make sure to put your bonnet on and leave it

on at all times. Do not answer the door if a stranger comes by. Do not leave the house. Keep the door locked."

Priscilla had heard all of this before but listened respectfully. When Willa felt she had covered everything she blew her daughter a kiss and was out the door.

Priscilla groaned inside, her mind now on Ollie. He had probably gone back to the castle by now. She tied on her bonnet, making sure it was secure, then waited, giving her mother ample time for a head start. Priscilla hoped if Ollie were there that he'd remain hidden. The blue baboon's presence would raise questions, questions that she was not yet ready to answer.

She tried to calm her worry, but the nagging voice inside Priscilla's head began to poke once more at her brain. It caused her to question her actions for a moment or two, but her final decision was soon made.

She would meet with Ollie.

"Hopefully, he's still there," she thought to herself.

She opened the door and stepped out into the

afternoon sun, locking the front entrance with a key that was always left under the mat. It was warm outside. She was already beginning to sweat around her hairline, but she didn't care. She ran across the clearing and for the second time that day ventured into the woods. Priscilla sensed a great adventure awaiting her, but she could never begin to imagine, even in her wildest dreams, the kind of unbelievable caper Ollie would plan.

15

Willa's Dilemma

"Just like a female," Ollie said in a loud, irritated voice. "They're always late. I'll give her just five more minutes."

Then he recalled what Priscilla had said, 'My parents are very protective.' Those had been her exact words. So, maybe," Ollie thought, "Priscilla found it impossible to break away or perhaps her mother refused to let her come."

He wondered if he should stay, and then in the distance he could hear someone singing. The voice was faint at first but grew louder and more distinct by the minute. Ollie could tell it was the voice of a lady, and he rather enjoyed listening to her happy, pleasant song. He relaxed in the lower hanging branches of the great oak peering through leaves as the woman came closer.

The mysterious traveler was now almost in full view. He caught a glimpse of her face as she turned her head in his direction for a brief second. He could see she was a red-haired lady. He waited for her to pass, but instead she stopped dead in her tracks, directly under the majestic oak. She began to look around, her voice now silent.

"She senses my presence," Ollie thought. It scared him to have her so close to his hiding spot. If he stretched his hand down from the leaves, he could almost touch her.

He dare not move, and though the leaves hid him, he prayed she wouldn't look up. He wondered who she was, and the longer he studied this stranger, the more certain he became that she did, indeed, remind him of someone, but whom? She turned her head again. Ollie could now see her face in full view. It was her eyes that revealed every-thing, and suddenly he knew: PRISCILLA!

The lady in the woods was Priscilla's mom. Ollie was sure of it.

"But, wait. That's impossible," he thought. "For this very attractive lady has red hair and everyone knows the law: no redhead can ever marry a blue-haired person." But, what if . . .

Suddenly all the clues came together: the hidden path, Priscilla's fear of discovery, Albert's worried look, his smile so much like that of his daughter and now the red-haired lady whose big green eyes were identical to Priscilla's. It all made perfect sense. They were a family, a family with a secret.

Ollie sat ever so still, his mind buzzed with this new found information, and the more he thought of his friend, the more he began to feel an over-whelming sense of loyalty. "So what if Priscilla's mom was married to a blue-haired guy? Big deal," he thought. "They're still the same people, aren't they? Their secret is safe with me."

He continued to watch her from his hiding place. Her big green eyes sensed danger as she scanned the surrounding forest. It was obvious to the blue baboon that this was a very sharp woman who had learned to trust her maternal instincts.

But now Ollie wished that she would move on. His joints were stiff and his muscles ached from sit-ting so still. Her thoughts, he could tell, were not for her own safety but for a daughter whom she believed was waiting securely in the shelter of her home.

"Is anyone there?" Willa called out.

The baboon held his breath.

Silence filled the forest.

"Perhaps Albert was right," thought Willa. "Perhaps I shouldn't leave Priscilla." She turned to go back, back toward home, back down the same path that her daughter was now traveling.

16

Mister Zotter

The castle square was packed with shoppers and visitors. It had been quite awhile since Willa had visited the market place. She was glad she had made the decision to come to the square instead of going home.

"My daughter is responsible and old enough to fend for herself," she kept repeating. Still, Willa's instincts left her somewhat uneasy.

Normally, Willa delighted in the hustle and bustle of the market place, but the atmosphere of this crowd and of the square in general had changed. There were no smiles, no warm greetings and no helping hands. There was a definite feeling of hostility as blue-hairs and redheads had clearly taken a stand against one another. It seemed as if an invisible line had been drawn in the sand. Willa could not understand the reason for such a division, for the moon was home to all its good people.

She decided to try a positive approach. She greeted everyone, red and blue-hairs alike, with a smile and a heartfelt "good afternoon." A few redheads returned her reply but blue-hairs merely grunted or said nothing at all. It seemed as if everyone was in a grumpy mood. The kings' hateful ways of thinking had poisoned the hearts and minds of the moon's once good and caring citizens.

Willa now understood Albert's fear and so she decided to hurry to the one place of business she knew she must visit: Mr. Zotter's Clock and Timepiece Shop. It was Willa's favorite store, and that was due in a large part to the gentle spirit of Mr. Zotter, himself.

Mr. Zotter was a kind and elderly gentleman who wore small, wire-rimmed, silver glasses at the end of his nose. He was bald except for a line of blue and gray hairs that extended from above each ear to the back of his aging head. He always wore a white, buttoned-down shirt with light brown knick-ers, and a simple vest. To this vest one couldn't help but notice a side pocket which contained an old silver timepiece that Mr. Zotter checked frequently throughout the day. He set all his clocks according to the time read on his old watch. It was his most prized possession for it had belonged to his father and his father before that.

The elderly clock maker had a very distinguished look about him. He was a true gentleman with a quiet wisdom. "Getting old is not so bad," Mr. Zotter would often say, "for age allows a person to finally appreciate the gift of time."

Yet, it was his wrinkled but delicate hands that were so fascinating to Willa. They had a feel for fixing the most intricate workings of a watch or clock so that each piece would keep perfect time. Mr. Zotter was a man who took great pride in his work. He was warm and friendly, and his little shop with its many different tick-tock sounds and varied chirpings of little cuckoos created a luring atmosphere.

Willa entered Mr. Zotter's place of business with a big, friendly smile. She ignored the presence of some blue-haired shoppers who turned up their noses, pointed fingers at her red hair and then mumbled insults under their breaths. Willa heard their "humphs" as they turned their backs in a snubbing way.

"Hello, Mr. Zotter. It's so good to finally see a warm, friendly face this afternoon," Willa said loud enough so that the rude shoppers could hear.

Mr. Zotter's face beamed. Willa was his favorite customer.

"It is so good to see you too, my dear," he replied, "and I think I know what brings you here."

"Why, I'm here to see you," Willa teased.

Mr. Zotter looked around then whispered, "Be careful, my dear, when using the *Why* word. I wouldn't want to get you into any trouble. He pointed secretly at his other blue-haired customers.

"Oh fiddlesticks," Willa answered but then was quick to add, "I appreciate your concern, Mr. Zotter. If you please, I'm here to pick up an engraved, pocket watch which I believe you've been holding for me. Here is my final payment."

"Thank you." He smiled then reached below the counter for Willa's long-awaited package. She opened the dark blue velvet box and examined its contents. The engraving on the inner side of the gold watch read:

One Day . . .
All my love, Willa

She was elated.

"Is it to your satisfaction?" old Mr. Zotter asked in a kind voice.

"It's perfect," Willa said. Her excitement grew as she continued to examine the quality of the elderly craftsman's work. In fact she became so engrossed with her husband's gift that she failed to see the growing number of ill-tempered blue-haired patrons entering Mr. Zotter's shop.

"He has no business selling to a redhead," they mumbled, "and she has no business standing on our side of the street."

Willa could feel their anger. She did not want to make things more difficult for the old watchmaker. So she decided to cut her visit short.

"The watch is absolutely perfect, Mr. Zotter," Willa said again, "and as much as I would love to visit with you, I must hurry on my way." She took his hand again and thanked him one last time.

But when Willa turned to leave, she found herself surrounded by irate, blue-haired customers.

"Some people don't know where they belong," stated a blue-haired lady, nudging Willa to the counter. "Perhaps she needs to be properly educated on what side of the square she needs to conduct her business."

"Please excuse me," Willa asked politely, holding tightly the watch she had just purchased. "Please, if you could just let me through."

"No, I don't think we will," said a large blue-haired lady.

Angry adults would not let her pass. They boldly blocked her way while holding the hands of their small children. These little ones watched intently and learned from the example set by their mothers and fathers.

The crowd had grown, making it impossible for Willa to leave. They began yelling insults and some even threatened her.

Mr. Zotter attempted to clear his shop of these troublemakers by asking them politely to leave, but no one would listen.

Willa's inner spirit then took over.

"You can't hold me here," she stated in a commanding voice. "I've done nothing wrong. I have my rights, so please let me through."

"Oh, a feisty one," several jeered. "She claims to have rights," others mocked.

Willa now felt crushed amid many blue-haired persons. She was afraid for she could see the hate and contempt in their eyes. They began to yell insults and even grabbed at her hair, loosening her precious comb. She reached, securing it in her hand before they could take it from her.

"What are you doing on this side of the square?" yelled a strong, familiar voice.

It was Albert. She could feel his muscular grip on her arm.

Willa looked into her husband's eyes and immediately knew the game she must play.

"I'm sorry, Sir," Willa now spoke in a meek and humble voice. "I wandered over to this side of the square. I apologize, and now, if you please, Sir, I would like to return to where I belong."

He squeezed her arm as if approving.

"All right then, break it up," Albert ordered. "I'll take care of this ignorant girl and escort her to where she needs to go. Break it up, I say."

The mob responded to the tall presence of this

blue-haired man. Albert then led Willa out of Mr. Zotter's shop to a narrow, secluded alleyway.

"Oh, Albert," Willa was shaking.

He looked all around to make sure no one else was present.

"I told you things were getting bad," Albert said. "The tension between the blues and the reds grows worse everyday. I want you to go home. Promise me that you and Priscilla will *not* come to the square for any reason. It's far too dangerous."

"Yes," Willa stated. "I understand."

"By the way," his eyes and voice softened, "did you find your anniversary gift?"

She opened her hand revealing the comb. "I would have fought tooth and nail to keep this precious gift," she said.

"I'm glad it didn't come to that," Albert said tightening his fists at the mere thought of someone hurting her. "You would have lost the comb and the battle."

Willa then opened her other hand.

"For you," she said. He carefully opened it, deeply touched by her meaningful gift. He read the engraving.

"Thank you so much, my darling," Albert said, hooking the chain of his new watch to his vest. "I will treasure it always."

Then looking around one more time to make sure they were alone, he held her face and kissed her.

"Hurry now," he said. "Get home to Priscilla and remember to stay in the cottage."

Willa nodded back, then whispered, "Be safe. I love you."

"And I you," he said with a soft voice.

Albert watched her cross over to the red side of the crowded square, where she was safe at least for the time being. He then turned ready to make his way back to the castle's main entrance. He took a deep breath, relieved that Willa was now on her way home and then came the mocking voice of the old fish lady.

17

The Old Fish Lady

"Well, well, well, you two sure looked awful chummy standing there," the old fish lady gloated. "You know the rule: no mixing or dating or congregating of red hairs with blues."

Albert's heart sank.

She stood there with her missing teeth, smiling as if she had just struck gold. Her blue hair was standing up on end, uncombed and in dire need of a shampoo. There were fish scales splattered on her face, in her hair and on her clothes. Her hands were stained and made rough from guts and grime. She wore a torn dirty dress with a smelly, fish-stained apron.

But none of this seemed to bother the old fish lady. She knew she had the "high and mighty" blue-haired man by the throat. There was no denying what she had just witnessed.

Albert was shocked. He had been so sure that no one was there in the alley with them. He looked around again and then noticed a broken-down cart.

"That's right honey," she purred at Albert. "You didn't bother to check on the other side of my old cart. I seen and heard it all. Normally, I don't come this way to make my deliveries of fresh fish for the kings' royal dinners, but the streets were so packed that I had to pull into this small alley to unload. I guess this is my lucky day," she snickered.

Albert stood in silence glaring at this conniving, old woman who now held the fate of his family in her hands.

"Say, what's your name, good-lookin'?" the fish lady cackled, sizing Albert up from head to toe.

She looked at him a little closer then smiled, amazed at her good fortune.

"Yes! I know who you are!" Her mind was spinning, her eyes full of excitement. "You're King Wynthor's servant," she beamed. "Then you must know better than anyone of my civic duty to report this little incident.

"Old Wynthor won't like this. No, he won't like it one bit, and neither will Norman," she continued. "It will mean certain banishment for you and the little missus. The kings will hold a public hearing, and everyone will have such fun watching you beg," taunted the old crone.

She thought about the power she now held over this handsome man. She would make him pay dearly for his disobedience.

"Now possibly," the fish lady toyed with Albert some more, "these old eyes could forget what they have just seen for a small price."

Albert seethed. She would play this incident for all it was worth.

Oh, why had he been so careless? He had jeopardized not only himself but his wife and daughter, too, and now there was yet another problem to contend with; he had no cash or coins to give, and he knew by the look on the fish lady's face that she would show him no mercy.

"I have no money," Albert said firmly.

"No, but you do have a brand new gold pocket watch, don't ya?" the old lady smirked. "Yup, I think a gold pocket watch would cover things quite nicely."

Albert reached into his pants pocket and attempted to give her his broken down timepiece. She cackled a long, irritating laugh.

"Just who do you think you're dealing with, mister?" the smelly old fish lady yelled. "I'm not stupid. Now give me the gold watch hooked to your vest, and give it to me now."

"Please, you don't know what this means to me," Albert pleaded.

"Nor do I care." She laughed again.

Albert stood firm, daring the cold-hearted woman to follow through with her threat.

"Okay," she said meeting his glare with her hateful eyes. "I guess it's time for a little announcement since you insist on making things difficult."

She stood on an old broken down bench that faced the street opening, "Hear ye', hear ye'," the fish lady called out. A few people walking by the alley looked her way.

Albert was tempted to call her bluff, but he knew the old fish lady did indeed have the upper hand. Her face held no feeling, no compassion, no hint of understanding for anyone but herself. There was no doubt in Albert's mind that this heartless old hag would go through with her threat, so he did the only thing he could do; he reluctantly unhooked his anniversary gift and placed it in the fish lady's dirty, greedy hand.

"Thank you, kind sir," she mocked him, "a pleasure doing business with ya'."

Anger raged within Albert's soul. He had fought hard to keep control of his temper, but now he fired a few conditions and threats of his own.

"Alright lady, you've just taken my most treasured possession. So know this, if you utter one word about me and what you have witnessed here today, I will personally hunt you down and expose some secrets about you. You see, I know how you cheat the royal chefs when they come to buy your 'fresh fish.' They pay for what they think is the 'catch of the day,' when in reality the fish you sell are five to seven days old. You would deny that of course, but I'll make sure you never sell another lobster or bluegill *ever*, so keep that wagging tongue of yours quiet. Do you understand?"

The fish lady's smirk was gone. She was afraid

of this blue-haired servant. She believed every word of his every threat. She stood there in the alley nervous and scared.

"I asked you a question!" Albert was trembling with anger. "Do you understand?"

"Yes sir," she mumbled, "you can count on me. Mums the word."

Albert looked at the old fish lady with disgust and then stomped back to the castle. His mind and heart were filled with thoughts of Willa and the sacrifices she must have made to purchase such a fine gift. He thought about his fellow citizens and their lack of concern for each other. He wondered how hate and disrespect had become the norm. He recalled the look of fear on Willa's face as she stood trapped in old Mr. Zotter's store, judged and ridiculed by others simply because her hair was red. It made no sense.

"How," he thought, "had things gone this far?" He worried about the kings' *Special Project* for Albert was certain it would cause only greater division. He thought of himself. What contributions had he made to make the moon a better place? None, he concluded.

Albert worked in a castle where he felt weak and disloyal to his own convictions. He answered to the ridiculous whims of a crazy king whose code of moral conduct was in direct conflict with his own. And now his worst fears were coming true.

Willa and Priscilla meant everything to him. They were his life, and he had put them in grave danger. He pondered all these things, and as he pondered, the burden became too much. He sat with his heavy heart on a cold, secluded castle step. He was tired and all alone, his soul full of sadness.

Unable to contain his feelings of failure and defeat, he put his head in his hands and allowed the flood of his own tears to wash upon his face.

18

The Plan

Priscilla found Ollie waiting in the lower limbs of the old oak. He made no mention of strangers, only that he had drifted off to sleep for a short period of time.

Priscilla couldn't believe her good fortune. Ollie must have been napping when Willa passed by on her way to the castle square.

The blue baboon observed the eyes of his friend. They were the eyes of the pretty lady who had just passed through, but, he could tell by Priscilla's averted glances that she was not yet ready to expose her family to anyone. He did not press her. She would reveal her secret in her own good time.

"Tell me about your morning," Priscilla said to Ollie. "I want to know more about regal life. What's the castle like? Are there beautiful handmaidens playing harps in the courtyards? Are there sweet smelling rose gardens and beautiful flowers everywhere?"

"Harps? Rose gardens? Flowers? Are you kidding?" Ollie almost laughed out loud. "Have you forgotten who's running the show up there within those castle walls? Our two psycho kings, Wynthor and Norman, remember? Hasn't your dad told you anything about the castle?"

"No, not the castle itself," Priscilla replied. "He gets very frustrated with the kings and shares those feelings with my mother, but my father doesn't like talking about work or the castle. So I try to picture it in my mind."

"Well, you can get those pretty little thoughts right out of your head," Ollie told her firmly, "because nothing like that exists nor will it ever exist as long as those two crazy kings are at their thrones. Never!

"Oh, by the way, I met your father today," Ollie said very matter-of-factly. "Cool guy."

"You did?" Oh no! Are you sure it was him?" Priscilla panicked.

"Oh, it was him all right. You have his smile."

"You didn't let on that you knew me, did you? Oh no! You did, didn't you?" Priscilla buried her face in her hands. "My parents will never trust me again."

"Good grief, Priscilla, get a grip," replied the baboon. "I didn't tell him anything. You asked me not to and so, as your friend, I honored your request."

Priscilla felt an immense relief and she threw her arms around Ollie.

"Oh, thank you," she said kissing him on the cheek.

"Okay! Okay! It's no big deal," he said, not really liking Priscilla's overt signs of affection. She pulled away and thanked him again.

"Say, you sure get worked up over your folks finding out certain things." Ollie said. "If my mom and dad were here, I'd tell them everything."

"One day, I too will share everything with my parents, but for now, I just can't." Priscilla responded.

"Well maybe you could share something with me," Ollie requested, "but it involves asking you a personal kind of *Why* question." He looked around, afraid that someone might overhear him.

Priscilla shrugged her shoulders, "Sure, go

ahead. Ask any *Why* question you want," she said. No one will hear you except for me and I'll never tell. What would you like to know?"

"Well, just out of curiosity, can you tell me *Why* you wear that bonnet on your head when it's eighty-eight degrees outside? Aren't you like boiling underneath? Let your hair down girl." He reached to untie the strings to her hair covering.

"No!" Priscilla moved away from him. "My bonnet stays on," she said in a commanding voice. "The answer to your question is simple. First of all, it's really none of your business, and secondly, I have my reasons. Case closed."

"Okay, okay," replied Ollie. "I'm cool with that. It was just a simple question. You don't have to snap my head off."

He could tell she meant business.

"Never ask a woman a personal question," the little baboon said to himself, "for it will only lead to trouble."

"I'm sorry," Priscilla apologized. "The truth is, I hate this bonnet."

"Then why wear it," asked Ollie?

"Like I said, I have my reasons," Priscilla answered sadly. "Someday, I'll explain everything."

"It's all right," Ollie said in a caring voice, "when you're ready, I'll be there."

Priscilla softened at his kind words. He really was a good friend.

They sat quietly for a minute or two, resting under the mighty oak. Then Ollie lit up as if someone had just shocked him with several hundred volts of electricity.

"Hey, Priscilla!" There was excitement in his voice. "I've got a great idea for an adventure. It's like the greatest idea I've ever had in my entire life."

"In your whole, entire life?" questioned Priscilla. This meant trouble. She was sure of it, but she would play along.

"An adventure?" she questioned. "It sounds very interesting. What kind of adventure?"

"A castle adventure."

"What do you mean by a castle adventure?" Priscilla asked. She wasn't following his train of thought very well.

"You and me, we'll go to the castle tonight."

"What? Are you crazy?" Priscilla couldn't believe what she had just heard.

Ollie's head was buzzing at the possibilities.

"I can show you around, share a little history of the place, show you some secret rooms and hall-ways. We'll have a great time!"

"I couldn't possibly," Priscilla said, shaking her head. But Ollie was deaf to her refusals. His eyes were bright, and one could almost see the wheels turning inside his head. I'll pick you up tonight, say around 11 o'clock? Your mom will have fallen asleep by then, right?"

He didn't wait for Priscilla to answer but continued on with his elaborate plan.

"We can swing to the castle. It doesn't take any time at all now that I can use my tail. We'll hang out. You can see where your dad works. There aren't any harps or rose gardens but one day that could all change. And you'll want to compare before and after pictures of the place. So, what do you say, friend? What a great adventure we could have."

He was out of breath just talking about this impossible caper. Priscilla's eyes grew big at the possibility of such a daring feat, and though she was tempted, she continued to shake her head no.

"I couldn't," she said.

"Sure you can," Ollie was persistent. "Let me ask you this, friend. When was the last time you were on an adventure?"

"I've never been on an adventure. Not really," Priscilla was a little embarrassed to admit it.

"Well, tonight's your big night then. It's the chance of a lifetime, a midnight caper. You'll never get another offer like this again. Never!"

Ollie could tell he was making some headway. Her eyes were bright with excitement. His enthusiasm was contagious. Priscilla was weakening.

"Well . . . well . . . Okay, I'll go."

"Hooray!" Ollie yelled. He could hardly contain his happiness and so he performed a series of cartwheels right there under the old oak.

Priscilla giggled.

"Prepare for some great fun," he announced.

"Now here is the plan," Ollie suddenly got serious. "I'll pick you up at the edge of the clearing at 11 o'clock. Don't worry, I'll protect you. All I ask is that you don't freak in the dark forest."

Priscilla frowned. "Just for the record," she interrupted, "I won't freak because I'm not afraid of the dark nor the forest, and for your information girls are every bit as brave as guys. Lastly, I don't need extra protection because I'm quite capable of taking care of myself, but I will meet you at the edge of the clearing. That way we can help find our way together."

Secretly she was very much relieved. She had never been in the woods alone at night.

Ollie knew this too, of course, but wasn't about to argue with her now. "I will have a lantern so I can signal you," he said.

"Okay," replied Priscilla, "but make sure you don't flash your light at my parent's bedroom window. You must keep very quiet. I wouldn't want my mother to wake.

"Oh dear," said Priscilla. "What about my father? He's working all night at the castle. What if he sees me?"

"He won't," said Ollie. "He'll need to take his place in the great chamber along with Wynthor and Norman and the rest of the servants. I'll need to make an appearance also, but I'll slip out. Wynthor will never know I'm gone.

"It's a meeting of both sides tonight. The kings plan to discuss their *Special Project,* and believe me it will drag on for hours. All servants, including your dad, will fall asleep, guaranteed. Your father will never know that you were even there."

"Do you know anything about this *Special Project* everyone is talking about?" Priscilla asked.

"As a matter of fact, I do," replied Ollie. "The two kings plan to paint red and blue lines in the sand around the whole moon in order to keep the redheads separated from the blues and vice versa. Crazy isn't it?"

"I'm afraid for us all," Priscilla said thoughtfully.

"So am I," said Ollie. "So am I."

19

The Decision to Go

Priscilla lay in her bed wide awake staring at the ceiling. Her hands were interlocked in a tight grip behind her neck, her lips firmly pressed. She was still fuming over her mother's treatment at the square. The entire scene, as described by Willa, played over and over again in Priscilla's mind. It made her mad, fighting mad.

"I feel like I could hit someone," she thought to herself, yet she knew that a raised fist rarely solved anything.

Priscilla thought about her father and wondered if he too might encounter danger. She wished with all her heart that he was home, safe and sound with his family. Priscilla loved her mother and father more than anything. They were good, honest people, kind and forgiving, but even kind and forgiving folks have their breaking points.

"They deserve better than this. It isn't fair," she thought, her eyes welling up with tears.

She looked at the clock sitting on her night stand. It was ten thirty. She could hear her mother sleeping soundly across the hall.

Priscilla pondered the day's events. She wondered if it was safe to venture out.

"Probably not," she thought.

Still, she felt compelled to go.

Her conscience had told her a thousand times that it was crazy to participate in a stunt like this. Priscilla agreed, but it seemed as if destiny was calling her.

She slipped into her jeans, pulled an old sweat-shirt over her head and tied up her tennis shoes. She thought of all the reasons why she should crawl back into bed. Then, securing her bonnet, she peeked in at her mother one last time, took a deep breath and made her final decision.

It was eleven o'clock. She was ready to go.

She walked out the front door, felt for the key, secured the lock and ran toward the secret path where Ollie now waited.

Part Three

Priscilla, she felt the whole moon could explode

Destroy every family and each small abode.

Each side, they were threatening, the kings would not bend

And life on the moon could now come to an end

For hate, it would poison the lives of them all

The blue-haired, the reds and the smallest of small.

20

The Adventure Begins

It was a perfect night. Millions of twinkling stars, each with its own unique light, created one great cosmic sea in which was nestled the famed sister moon. It sat in the clear northern sky, poised in its orbit.

Priscilla stopped in the clearing as if hypnotized by the beauty that now surrounded her. She barely noticed Ollie who had ventured from the path to join her. The two unlikely friends watched in quiet, reverent awe as countless moonbeams traveled through distance and time, exploding into prisms of gorgeous light.

"It's beautiful." Ollie said in a soft voice.

"Yes," Priscilla whispered. "Look! See how the glow lights up the deepest part of the forest?" At this she remembered her father's words: "Once you've seen it, there's no mistaking from where it came."

Priscilla smiled. She slowly began to understand. The mysterious light came from above. It came from a Power greater than anyone or anything, and it filled not only the night sky but the inner sanctum of Priscilla's own heart.

She closed her eyes and savored its peaceful warmth. The warmth mysteriously kindled a new kind of freedom within her, a spiritual freedom that lifted from her burdened shoulders, all those things that prevent joy and healing and growth of spirit.

She smiled at her blue-haired friend and wondered if he had felt the same kind of experience. She no longer sensed the deep anger she had harbored just a short time ago. She was content, for she knew that a higher Power would now guide, protect and lead them to where they needed to go.

Ollie, excited to get started, took Priscilla's hand, and they ran to the great oak. He helped her to his back and started his climb.

"All aboard," he called to his only passenger. "I

advise you to hang on tight for you're about to travel at the speed of light." He carried a lantern which he handed to Priscilla for safe-keeping.

She didn't know why but she felt an unexplainable confidence in her navigator and didn't know whether to call it blind stupidity or blind faith. She only knew how exciting it was to experience something different with a friend who was fun and ready to have a good time.

He skillfully maneuvered through the trees while singing his favorite hit songs. He would whack Priscilla on top of her head with a gentle thump of his tail when it was time for her to join in the chorus. He clearly loved music and had a natural talent for it. Priscilla enjoyed his voice and did a few, funky moves with her arms as they traveled along. In her whole life, she had never felt this lighthearted or carefree, and so she watched with great anticipation as the castle came into full view.

But as they neared their destination her excitement dwindled for the castle, and all its grounds appeared cold and gloomy. The prisms of light barely reflected here.

She looked down and noticed how high they were.

"Don't we want ground level when we land?" she asked Ollie.

"That's a negative," he replied in his best pilot voice. "A large tree branch overhangs the fourth floor balcony. We will enter the castle there and work our way down." Priscilla watched as Ollie skillfully worked his way through the final trees before coming to a gentle stop.

"Please gather all your belongings and exit left and thank you for flying *Baboon Airways*, the airways with a special *tail* wind that gets you there on time, every time. Get it, Priscilla . . . *tail* wind? Get it?" he said again putting his tail to her face.

"I get it," Priscilla laughed. But when she looked at her surroundings, she was instantly afraid, for the castle loomed dark and ugly and yet powerful. It was dirty and had a foul smell. Ollie could see the distaste on her face.

"Sorry, but I didn't have time to dust or vacuum," he said jokingly.

Priscilla half grinned. She didn't want to seem apprehensive, but there was something very spooky about this place. Her eyes peered all around. She could see a high overhead dome extending over the top floor. Underneath the dome were many rafters, and though it was dark, Priscilla thought she could see something hovering high in the blackness. She took a couple of steps then stopped. "Did you hear something?" she whispered, her eyes and ears alert.

"Nah, I didn't hear a thing," Ollie reassured her. "There's nothing here to fret about. Oh, once in a while, a bat flies by, but they're small and harmless."

"Bats? There are bats lurking around?" Priscilla questioned in a shaky voice.

"Maybe one or two," said Ollie. "Say, you're not afraid of a little old bat, are you?"

The question was barely out of his mouth when a big, bold, dive-bombing bat swooshed down past Ollie, touching his nose. Within a few seconds another sonar-driven creature, much larger than the first, buzzed not only at Ollie but at Priscilla as well.

Ollie, clearly shaken, dove to the floor and covered his face.

Priscilla lifted the lantern. She could see hundreds of beady-eyed bats perched in the rafters waiting to make their move.

She called out in a sing-song voice, "Oh, Ollie."

She could feel his shaking body next to her foot. "We have a major problem, my friend. You know those one or two harmless bats that occasionally fly by? Well, they're having a major, family reunion, and I don't think we're invited. So, if it's okay with you, I suggest that we get out of here as quickly as we can. But you will need to show the way."

"I don't think I can," whimpered Ollie. "I have a terrible fear of bats."

"You had a terrible fear of heights just this morning," Priscilla reminded him. "Remember how you conquered that fear rather quickly. I'm sure you can conquer your fear of bats as well and Ollie," she continued.

"Yes," he responded with a shaky voice.

"The sooner, the better."

She heard the flapping of wings again and spotted the same large, daring bat swooping down on Ollie.

"Stay away from my friend, you blood-sucking varmint," Priscilla called out.

"This is embarrassing," Ollie thought, "a girl defending me." I have to pull myself together, and I have to do it fast!"

But when he lifted his head he nearly fainted at the sight of so many bats gathered.

He slowly stood. It was time to muster every ounce of courage. "We need to formulate a plan," he said, terrified.

"And we need to formulate it fast," Priscilla interjected.

The bats were growing bolder by the second, swooping and screeching and flapping their wings. Priscilla felt she might panic but knew that a successful escape from this predicament rested mainly on her shoulders. She had to keep a clear head and so she scanned all sides of the balcony. It was dark and difficult to see until her eyes focused on a flickering light made visible through an open door in the east wall.

"Where does that door lead to?" She asked Ollie.

He uncovered his face and stared at Priscilla's observation. "Yes!" he answered. "That door leads to a stairwell which connects the four main castle floors. It's our way out! I remember, now. I propped open each door and placed a lit torch outside the fourth floor entrance before coming to your house. I guess fear made me forget."

For a moment Ollie felt almost heroic, but as he peered across the large open balcony, his mind began to panic once more. "The door looks so far away," he stammered while dodging bats that were coming at him from all directions. His courage was dwindling. Priscilla could hear it in his voice and see it in his trembling face. He stood frozen, unable to move.

"We need to make a run for it," Priscilla told him. Ollie nodded his head in agreement but continued to stand motionless. "Take my hand," Priscilla ordered. He reached and placed his left hand in hers while covering his eyes with his right.

More bats hovered overhead. "Ollie, uncover your eyes," Priscilla commanded impatiently. "You've got to see where you are going, don't you?" He did as she instructed hanging onto her every word.

"Now, as soon as we reach the door," Priscilla

told him, "we will need to close it quickly. We must work together."

"Okay," said Ollie. "I'm with you."

The bats were getting more aggressive. They now slapped the heads of this small girl and her strange friend with black expanded wings. "We're getting out of here *now!*" Priscilla screamed. But the sound of so many bats screeching at once was deafening. Ollie could not hear her, and so she faced him and pointed to the door.

"Ready, set, go!" she yelled at the top of her lungs. They ran as fast as their legs would carry them, dodging their black-winged attackers.

"*Go! Go! Go!*" Ollie screamed. They were almost to the door when he lost Priscilla's hand. He turned and saw her slip to the dirty floor. Frenzied bats circled over her. She hung tight to her bonnet while crying out, "Ollie! Help me, please!" This time, unlike the morning, there was no hesitation.

"Leave my friend alone!" Ollie yelled. And he found within himself a hidden strength. He would not allow these nasty, black demons of the night to hurt her, and so he grabbed her hand and pulled her through the door entrance with no regard for his own safety. With gripped torch in hand, he then warded off any daring bats that tried to escape while he and Priscilla closed the oak door together.

For a few minutes more bat sounds continued to echo from the other side until finally, all was quiet, the last of the black-winged creatures giving up their cause.

Priscilla and Ollie sat on the cold, castle steps, grateful for a few moments rest, for they were both emotionally and physically drained.

"I never want to go through that again," Priscilla shivered at the thought.

Ollie calmly reassured her, "You have nothing to fear but fear itself, my dear."

"Is that a fact?" she smiled.

"Yes, that's a fact!" Ollie said with certainty. "Feel free to quote me, if you'd like."

He leaned his back against the cold wall of the stairwell.

She knew his brave act at the end of their ordeal had taken much courage on his part. "Thank you, Ollie, for saving my life. Again."

The blue baboon smiled then stood up with his

chest out and his head held high, proud of his heroic deed.

"Think nothing of it," Ollie replied. "Besides, what are friends for if they can't save each other once in awhile?"

Priscilla smiled at his words. "Yes," she thought. "I guess we all need saving at different times of our lives." And she rose up with new-found energy, ready now to continue this "Great Adventure" with Ollie leading the way.

21

The Rat Race

Priscilla felt engulfed by the darkness. It seemed as if the entire stairwell had plunged into an abyss.

Ollie noticed her apprehension. He took her hand, then guided her slowly but surely down each step until finally the two friends stood facing the oak door that would allow entry to the third floor.

"You're going to love this," the blue baboon said, while propping his torch against the stairwell wall. "But you will need to use your imagination to envision what this part of the castle looked like years ago. At one time it was beautiful, or so I've been told."

Priscilla grew anxious. She took a couple of steps forward, eager to enter. But Ollie held her back.

"Uh, before we go in, there is one, tiny, little

thing I should mention." Ollie said with some hesitation.

Priscilla looked suspicious. "I'm listening," she replied.

"Well, I don't want to scare you off," the blue baboon stated, "but we may run into one or two little mice on the other side of this door. And since all girls freak at the sight of a little, old mouse, I thought I'd better prepare you."

Priscilla began to laugh. "After our fourth floor experience with those crazy bats, I don't think a couple of little mice will scare me off." But secretly she detested any kind of rodent. "Hopefully," she thought, "any wayward mouse would stay hidden."

They entered, closing the door behind them. Slowly they scanned the mysterious room. The lantern, now held by Ollie, revealed a magnificent, dusty, old, crystal chandelier hanging from the middle of a high, ornate ceiling, and though miles of intertwining spider webs made it difficult to see, Priscilla could almost imagine the fixture reflecting soft glows of evening light.

"How beautiful it must have been," she thought.

Stained-glass windows, dulled from dust and

lack of cleaning, extended up the outside walls from the marble floor to the ceiling. Torn, velvet chairs and small tables covered with lacy linens lined the main floor of this once spectacular room. There were beautiful hand-painted vases with withered roses still remaining. The room seemed mysteriously frozen in time. And then suddenly, it was all very clear.

"This was once the castle ballroom," Priscilla whispered.

She closed her eyes for just a moment and imagined herself dancing in a beautiful gown with a handsome prince, her purple hair exposed for all to see. She swayed back and forth smiling to herself.

"What are you doing?" Ollie asked.

"Dancing," she replied.

"Dancing with whom?"

"With the most handsome prince ever seen on this moon," Priscilla said. Her voice was now dreamy. "Can't you see him?" He's right here leading me across this beautiful floor."

Ollie looked around. He, of course, saw no one. "The girl is cracking up," he thought. "Maybe this adventure thing wasn't such a good idea after all."

The squeaking sound brought her back to reality. "What's that noise?" she asked, afraid of his answer.

She could see Ollie's face as he stooped to illuminate the floor of this magnificent room. His eyes, now big as saucers, looked directly at Priscilla.

"Rats," he said, "hundreds and hundreds of rats. She wanted to scream but couldn't. Ollie was equally afraid.

"One or two little mice, uh?" Priscilla posed the question with a hint of sarcasm. She felt her heart racing as hundreds of flea-infested, long-tailed, squealing rats were now pouring in from every crack and crevice on the third floor.

"We must get out of here." Priscilla pleaded in a quiet, terrified voice.

She waited for Ollie's response.

"I can't believe the size and numbers of these rats," he said frozen. "Where did they all come?"

"How should I know," Priscilla snapped back at him.

"You don't have to yell at me," he said in a hurtful tone. "Can't you see that I have this . . . "

"Terrible fear of rats?" Priscilla finished his sentence.

"How did you know?" Ollie was surprised.

"Oh, just a lucky guess," she told him but then added firmly, "We need a plan, Ollie, and we need it *now!*"

It made her nervous to rely on her blue-haired friend with his limited courage, but she had no choice. She knew nothing of castle rodents. Her fate was in his hands.

"A plan, a plan," Ollie repeated as he stood next to Priscilla thinking out loud. His knees were shaking. So were hers.

Bold, unafraid rats now covered the entire third floor.

"I've never seen anything like this before." Ollie said in a quivering voice. "This is unbelievable."

"The plan, Ollie, the plan," Priscilla had once again reached the peak of her patience.

"Oh yes, the plan," he repeated again. "Okay, I know just what we'll do," he finally said in a take-charge tone.

"You do?" Priscilla said, shocked.

"Well, don't act so surprised," he said, a little irritated. "I'm an expert when it comes to plan making, and further more, I know just what to do in this unfortunate situation."

Priscilla was all ears. "Well, let's hear it," she said.

"We must move very slowly and very carefully to the stairwell," he told her. "And above all, we mustn't panic. These critters seem very jumpy to me, and it won't take much to set them off into a wild stampede. Now hold my tail and walk slowly behind me." She did as Ollie instructed but still the rats kept coming. They were gaining in numbers and at times would stop to sniff her shoes, daring her to move on. She wanted to run but continued to follow Ollie's lead.

Inch by inch, the two friends moved slowly across the floor, taking one baby step at a time. But just as Priscilla sensed her fear easing a bit, she was horrified to feel the claws of a large rat now clinging to her back. She froze as the rodent made its way to her shoulder blades. She felt its warm, revolting breath on the back of her neck. Priscilla thought she might get sick, but somehow she managed to keep her supper and her panic inside.

She called to Ollie in a weak voice. He turned and looked with wide, frantic eyes. The rat now sat on top of Priscilla's head, its long tail slithering down inside her sweatshirt. She felt it moving back and forth on her bare back.

"Keep coming," Ollie coached her, "and don't panic!" They continued to make headway with the rat still delicately balanced. For once, Priscilla was glad for her bonnet.

"Take it nice and slow," Ollie said in a shaky voice. "We're almost there," but when he looked back, he could see that Priscilla had taken matters into her own hands. She now had her rat by the tail. It dangled in midair lunging at her with bared teeth and a wild look of fury on its hissing face.

Ollie watched in disbelief as Priscilla now swung the crazed rat over her head like a cowgirl with a lasso.

He yelled, "No!"

But it was too late. With one last swing, Priscilla let go, flinging the miserable, squealing rodent against the north wall of the ballroom. The splat diverted the faster, stronger rats for a few seconds. They raced across the floor and began feeding on the dead carcass. Other rats, now set in motion, united themselves in one mad stampede.

"Run!" Priscilla heard Ollie's voice. She headed toward the entrance door sprinting as fast as she could go, but the mad charge of the countless, horrid creatures surrounded her again. She felt she might go mad for beneath the soles of her shoes was the gross feel of trampled rats, their forced-out guts sending other rats into a feeding frenzy.

She panicked in the darkness yelling Ollie's name.

"Over here," he called. He somehow opened the door and was fighting off infested rats with the torch he had set outside the ballroom entrance.

"Hurry!" He pleaded, "I can't hold them off much longer."

Priscilla felt as if she couldn't go on. The high-pitched squeals of crazed rats created a loud and frightening echo that added to the chaos.

She heard Ollie call again. He needed her. She closed her eyes in an attempt to free her mind of the bedlam that surrounded her.

"Help me!" she cried as she sprang forward in one, last, desperate leap of faith. Then mustering all the strength left within, Priscilla closed the heavy oak door, sealing off the rat's only way of escape while Ollie put the torch to those few, daring rodents who happened to slip through. One touch of his flame to their coarse, ugly hair sent them into a mad, convulsive fit.

Their ordeal now over, Priscilla sat on a third floor step. She was grateful for her brave, blue-haired friend. He had saved her again.

"Thank goodness for your lit torch," Priscilla said.

"Think nothing of it," Ollie's voice was shaking. "It's all in a day's work."

She grinned at her three-time rescuer. She was impressed with his planning skills. It was an ugly castle with horrid, frightening creatures but that wasn't his fault. He was trying very hard to show her a good time and for that, she was grateful. But she was becoming increasingly concerned.

"How do I get back home?" she questioned Ollie. We certainly can't go back the way we came. We barely made it through the first time."

"No need to worry," Ollie replied. "I'll come up with a plan. Trust me.

"By the way," he continued. "Remind me never to put my tail down your back. That rat never knew what hit him."

Priscilla smiled a rather proud smile. "It was a pretty good throw, wasn't it?" she said, grinning at Ollie. But her whole body shivered with disgust when she recalled the incident. She wished she could erase it from her mind.

Secretly, she worried about Ollie's plan for her return.

What if it faltered? What if she was forced to face the perils of the third and fourth floors again?

"I guess I will cross that bridge when I come to it," she said to herself.

Little did she know that destiny had its own plan, a plan that would force Priscilla to search within her own heart for a special hidden courage she had yet to realize.

22

The Second Floor

Two hallways, one red and one blue, led to the private quarters of the two kings. Ollie led Priscilla down Wynthor's hallway first. Here she observed many, enlarged, framed pictures hanging on the walls.

"Who is that?" Priscilla cried out.

"That, my dear, is our own King Wynthor."

The sight of Wynthor posing in his bathing suit caused Priscilla to laugh out loud.

"Hey, Priscilla, what do you think of this sexy pose?" She looked to see Ollie standing in the hallway near a large picture of King Wynthor. Her blue-haired friend was flexing his small biceps and throwing out his blue-haired chest. He had a strained, grunted look on his face, like that of a professional wrestler. Ollie then proceeded to mimic other poses, flexing his triceps and hamstrings and back muscles. The blue baboon was hilarious in his interpretations of the kings, and Priscilla laughed until she cried.

He then directed her to Wynthor's bedroom. Everything was blue, the walls, ceilings and floors, the bedspread, the sheets, the furniture. It was a boring room. In fact, it was probably the ugliest, most boring room Priscilla had ever seen in her whole life. She noticed Wynthor's many picture frames with photos of only himself. "How sad," she thought, "not to have a picture in your room of someone other than yourself."

Ollie then led Priscilla down the red wing of the second floor where she viewed Norman in the same poses. He had the exact same bedroom, only in red and his picture frames, like Wynthor's, contained photos only of himself.

Having checked out the major part of the second floor, it was time to move on.

"We've got lots to do and things to see," said Ollie. He showed no signs of fatigue.

As they descended to the first floor, Priscilla

could hear the muffled, faint sounds of voices. They were angry voices.

"Are those the kings arguing?" she asked.

"Yes indeed," answered Ollie. "Next stop, the first floor. You are now about to enter the great chamber room. Follow me."

23

The First Floor

The first floor, like the others, was dark and gloomy. Yellow wax slowly dripped from old candles that lit the hallway. The dim light from the candles created huge, spooky shadows of Ollie and Priscilla. These shadows gave to the first floor a creepy, eerie feeling.

The walls were covered with dozens of hand-painted portraits of both kings, but unlike the comical pictures she had just seen, these portraits attempted to show off the kings' more regal, stately side. They depicted Norman and Wynthor sitting high on their respective thrones, their crowns in place and their fancy, velvet robes draped off their royal shoulders. Each tried to outdo the other by wearing expensive jewels around their necks and ornate rings on their fingers.

Priscilla was not impressed. "It takes a lot more than jewels and fancy robes to make a good ruler," she said, using her father's words.

"What's that awful smell?" she asked Ollie as they neared the royal chamber.

"Oh gee, I almost forgot, you'll need one of these," and he handed Priscilla a padded clothespin that he had clipped to his tail for safe keeping.

"What in the world is this?" she asked, bewildered.

"It's my fantastic new invention," said Ollie. "It will protect your nose from the stench-filled air caused by the expelled, internal gases of our two regal kings. Their exploding rear ends have been honking and tooting all night long. You'll thank me for my little invention when I open the chamber room door. I call it my Super-Duper-Nose-Closer. It normally sells for just three dollars and ninety-nine cents, but for you, well, let's just call it a gift from a friend."

"Gosh," said Priscilla, "I've never received a gift like this before."

"Of course not, silly," Ollie beamed. "The Super-Duper-Nose-Closer is one of kind. All the servants have one. Let me show you how it works."

He took his time in placing his own nose closer. He sniffed and snuffed and adjusted and repositioned the device over and over again till he found it to his liking. Priscilla watched intently. "I wonder if he knows how funny he looks," she thought.

"Now, you may wonder just how this device works on smaller noses," Ollie said. "Well, let me take just a few moments of your time and show you."

Priscilla looked around. No one else was present, but Ollie talked as if he had a whole audience in front of him.

"Could I have a volunteer, please?" he asked.

She raised her hand cautiously.

"This is your lucky day, little girl," he said taking Priscilla by the arm.

"Now as you can see," Ollie addressed his invisible crowd, "my shnoz is much bigger than the shnoz of this small girl, but look how easy my invention adjusts."

"You see," he informed Priscilla, "one size fits all. I just pull a little left this way and readjust to the right this way and *Voila!* The Super-Duper-Nose-Closer fits you like a charm. There, how does that feel?" he asked Priscilla, his face full of pride.

"It feels perfect," she lied with her new nasal voice.

"Isn't it amazing," Ollie continued to beam.

"It's pretty amazing, alright."

"Well, if you ever need another one, just let me know," Ollie said. "You might want to consider getting one for your mom. It makes a great gift."

"I'm sure it does," replied Priscilla. "They certainly are unique."

With their nose closers in place, the brave duo made their way to the royal chamber.

"Shh!" whispered Ollie. "We must proceed in silence."

He and Priscilla secured their nose closers one last time and then slowly walked down the dreary hallway. The kings' voices grew steadily louder while Priscilla grew steadily more anxious.

"What if they see us," she whispered in Ollie's ear.

"Shh!" Ollie said again. "Keep quiet!"

They had come to the great chamber door. Ollie took hold of the knob and very carefully turned it while pushing the door ever so slowly.

"I'm actually going to see the kings," Priscilla

thought to herself. She didn't know why, but she was actually excited. They were, after all, celebrities of a sort. She felt as if she were part of some historical moment.

The chamber room door opened slightly. Priscilla gasped for it was her father who she saw first.

He was sleeping, just as Ollie had predicted, but he looked very uncomfortable with his head resting on a hard, wood table. Ollie gave Priscilla a stern look. He firmly held a finger to his lips to signal absolute silence. And then, very carefully, he opened the door wider to reveal the entire chamber scene.

Priscilla immediately noticed the foul odor even with her padded clothespin in place. She could see that each servant wore one of Ollie's devices which forced them to sleep with their mouths wide open. The snoring combined with the passing of royal gases, created a very weird and unpleasant sound that not only affected her ears but her nose as well.

She observed Rodney next. He snoozed on the floor not far from King Norman's feet. He, too, had a Super-Duper-Nose-Closer secured between his facial whiskers. He actually looked rather cute, thought Priscilla, but as she stared at him more closely, she detected a teasing, mischievous smile that was evident even as he slept.

Lastly, Priscilla looked upon King Norman and King Wynthor. She studied them as they faced each other over a long table that was painted half red and half blue. They were head to head, stubborn and refusing to listen.

"My *Special Project*," Wynthor smirked, "will at last isolate all redheads from the richer, more saintly blues. Painted lines in the sand will symbolize my sole reign, but the official proclamation as to why I am the obvious ruler will be decreed by my senior servant. It will come at the eleventh hour. So beware, Norman, for when the clock strikes, I will show no mercy toward any redhead and that includes you."

His voice was suddenly low-pitched with a dark, threatening tone that made Priscilla shiver. But the red-haired king was not intimidated.

"The power of the moon is mine!" Norman screeched, and his high pitched screech nearly caused Priscilla and Ollie to jump out of their shoes.

"The *Special Project* was my idea," the red-haired king continued, "and once that project is complete, I will issue a new law. But for now know this: the moon belongs to the strong and the mighty. The moon belongs to the more superior mind. The moon belongs to me!"

"Bah!" shouted Wynthor.

And their talk of power and contempt would continue well into the wee hours of the morning, of that Priscilla was sure.

"Don't they ever get tired of arguing?" She wondered.

She looked at her father again and felt an overwhelming sense of sadness. He was trapped in a place that was so unlike his inner self, and she wished with all her heart that she could free him.

Ollie silently signaled Priscilla that it was time to go. She found herself eager to leave. The constant passing of inner gas was gross and made for a very stinky chamber. She was amazed at how her father and other servants managed to sleep through the tooting, the stench and the screaming.

"I guess a person can get used to just about anything," thought Priscilla.

She very quietly assisted Ollie in closing the great chamber door unaware of Rodney, the cat, who was now awake and formulating a caper all his own. He lay quietly with one eye open and a sinister smile on his cold and calculating face.

"Who was that girl?" the mean old cat wondered. "And what was she doing with King Wynthor's baboon?

"Well, whoever she is," Rodney chuckled, "tonight will be a night she'll never forget."

24

Secrets Shared

"We pulled it off," Ollie said, jumping for joy once they could no longer hear the kings' voices. His excitement led him to perform a whole series of cartwheels while Priscilla cheered and applauded.

"I told you I'd get you into their chamber. I promised a great adventure, and I delivered," Ollie bragged. "What a great night! Oh, we may have started off a little rough, but in the end you must admit that this caper is the most awesome caper you've ever had!"

She felt no need to remind him that this was the only caper she had ever had. But if she experienced a thousand other adventures, she was quite sure that none would ever compare to this one.

"Stick with me kid," Ollie said, "and you'll never go wrong. We need to celebrate!"

"It was great to have a friend," thought Priscilla. Though she didn't particularly like the castle's moldy walls and funny smells, she had to admit that she did have fun outrunning bats and flinging rats and mimicking funny poses of their spineless leaders. She couldn't believe that Ollie had dared to open the great chamber door. She could now say that she had actually seen the two crazy kings in the flesh, and though she felt some sadness for her father, she did feel proud of her courage. Ollie had even given her a free gift—his Super-Duper-Nose-Closer. Maybe she would get one for her mother.

"And the night is still young," Ollie joyously proclaimed.

"What's next?" Priscilla asked with an excited voice.

"Come along, friend," Ollie said. "It's time to get reenergized. I'm rather hungry, aren't you?"

"Well now that you bring it up," said Priscilla. "I'm starving."

Two massive kitchens, one colored blue and one colored red, served each individual king. Priscilla could tell that Ollie had conducted many night time raids such as this before. He knew the location of everything as he went from cupboard to cupboard and fridge to fridge to see what goodies were available.

"Hmmm," the blue baboon muttered, "let's see what we have here."

Priscilla sat on a small stool and watched her friend examine the possibilities.

"I've got left over lobster tails and a few bluegills," Ollie informed his castle guest. "Does fish strike your fancy?"

She had no desire to eat cold fish. So she asked him, "Would you by chance have any regular food, like some peanut butter and jelly?"

"My thoughts exactly," stated Ollie, and he raided both kitchens retrieving everything he needed.

Priscilla waited patiently. She listened as Ollie hummed a tune while spreading thick coats of peanut butter and jelly on slices of homemade bread. Then pressing the covered slices together so that the combination of jelly and peanut butter oozed from all sides, he said, "Dinner is served my lady."

"Thank you," she said taking a big bite.

"What would you like to drink?" asked Ollie. "I've got red wine or wine out of a blue bottle."

"How about a plain old glass of milk," Priscilla said with a grin.

"Coming right up," Ollie replied. He was rather surprised at how much he enjoyed waiting on her. They ate in silence for a minute or two before Priscilla spoke in a serious tone.

"I want to thank you, Ollie, for all you've done tonight. You've been a great host. But I must admit, I was rather frightened in the chamber, because I finally realized something very important: our moon is in trouble, big trouble. The kings are dangerous. There's no telling what they might do. Painted lines in the sand will only increase the tensions and the hate between our citizens. People could get hurt. Someone needs to stand up to Norman and Wynthor."

"Well," Ollie stated, "that would take a full-fledged hero, a special person with a lot of guts. I'd do it myself because, well, you already know what a brave, gutsy, hero-like kind of guy I am, but, uh, well, my voice doesn't carry very well and so I would recommend that you find someone else to address the two kings."

"That's okay, Ollie," Priscilla said. "The voice needs to come from the people. Maybe one day, such a person will step forward."

She smiled at her blue-haired friend as she plopped the last piece of sandwich into her mouth and drank the remaining portion of her milk. She knew he was pretty much a chicken inside, but still, she felt a deepening kinship with this funny, yet very feeling creature.

She had just started on the kitchen cleanup when Ollie took her hand and pulled her aside.

"Forget all that and come with me," he said. "I've got a great idea."

She willingly followed him, wondering what he had in mind and where he was taking her.

"There's something I simply must show you. It's my most special place in the entire world."

His torch no longer carried any flame so he reached for the lantern held now in Priscilla's hand. He would need it to light their way. But Priscilla held back. "Are there rats or bats or other creatures

169

that I need to know about before we go any further?" she asked him.

"Not where we're going," Ollie replied truth-
fully.

She surrendered the lantern and followed the
blue baboon through the pantry door. Together
they stood at the base of what appeared to be
another endless flight of narrow, winding stairs.

"We're going up there?" Priscilla asked.

"Yup," he said. "Follow me."

Ollie led the way with Priscilla at his heels.
When they finally reached the top, Priscilla saw
another small door.

"Close your eyes," Ollie ordered.

She did as she was told, allowing herself to be
led out into the cool night air. Refreshed by the
summer breeze, Priscilla asked again, "Can I open
my eyes now?"

"Not yet."

He led her by the hand to the rail of a small
balcony.

"Now!" he said.

Priscilla gasped at the view before her.

"We are at the highest point of the highest tower in the castle," Ollie said with pride.

Priscilla gazed out at all that was before her. This was by far the best part of her "Great Adventure." She felt as if she could reach out and touch the stars. Everything seemed right with the world.

Dim street lights allowed her to look down on the villages below. She could see rows of houses along cobbled streets and she wondered about the families residing within.

She closed her eyes again.

"It feels so peaceful here," Priscilla said. "I can almost forget the problems of our moon."

Ollie then came to stand by her.

"That's why I love this place," he said. "It helps me forget about my own loneliness, at least for a little while. It may sound a little strange, but it's here where I feel close to my family, and it's here where I dream about my future and what I'd like to be one day."

"What would you like to be?" Priscilla asked most sincerely.

Ollie turned his face away and looked down.

"I'm kind of embarrassed to say," he was suddenly shy. "You're going to think it's silly."

"No, I won't. I promise. Tell me. Please," Priscilla begged.

"Well, okay," Ollie decided to take a chance.

He took a deep breath.

"I'd like to be a professional harmmmm . . . player." His words were muffled, trapped inside his throat.

"What?" asked Priscilla, "Can you speak up? I can't hear you."

"I said I'd like to be a professional harmmmmm . . . player."

"I still can't understand what you're saying," Priscilla said, "Just spit it out."

"I said I'd like to be a professional harmonica player!" Ollie yelled out. "There, I've said it. See, I knew you'd think it was a crazy idea. Whoever heard of a blue baboon playing a harmonica?"

"Well, I will admit," responded Priscilla, "I've never heard of a blue baboon playing a harmonica before but that doesn't mean it couldn't happen. As a matter of fact, now that I think about it, I think you'd make a great harmonica player."

Ollie was elated. He didn't know why but her supportive words meant a lot to him.

"Do you really think so?" he asked excitedly.

"Absolutely," she said, "I think you should pursue your dream."

Priscilla looked back at the night sky. This Great Adventure was so far, a huge success.

"Okay," Ollie said, turning to Priscilla, "now it's your turn. What would you like to be?"

She gave no answer.

"Come on," he coaxed, "I won't laugh. It will be our little secret. I promise not to tell a soul."

Priscilla continued to ponder in the moonlit sky. She remembered her mother's words: "Sometimes fear and lack of courage allows the madness to continue."

She believed in the truth of those words.

"There comes a time to let go of one's fear," she thought. Maybe this was the time. Maybe this was the place. She turned and faced Ollie. Her words were simple, her voice calm.

"I would like a chance to be me," she said.

Then slowly, without hesitation, she removed her bonnet and allowed the soft, thick tresses of her purple hair to cascade around her face.

25

The Response

Ollie fell back, his mouth open, his face expressing disbelief. She was different all right, maybe too different.

Why hadn't he thought of this possibility before? "Of course," he said, "red and blue make purple."

"That's right," stated Priscilla. "My mother has red hair."

"Yes, I know," said Ollie. "I saw her walking through the forest today."

"But, you said you were sleeping," she responded.

"That's because I wanted you to share your family secret when you were ready. I had no idea that you were the biggest secret of all."

He had a million *Why* questions but was hesitant to ask.

Priscilla didn't know how to interpret his surprise. He stammered as he backed away, "I don't know what to say. Your hair . . . it's just so . . . it's just so . . .

"Different?" Priscilla filled in the word.

"Yeah," said Ollie, "I guess that's the word all right."

His head began spinning with a host of confusing thoughts and emotions. He could get into big trouble hanging out with a purple-haired person. If the kings got wind of this, they'd banish him right along with her and her family.

Priscilla studied her blue-haired friend.

"What are you thinking?" she asked. "You seem so uncomfortable and yet I'm still the same person, aren't I?"

"Sure," said Ollie, trying to convince her. "Everything's cool."

He avoided her eyes, fearful that she would somehow read his mind. Priscilla took a deep breath. She was afraid to ask the next question, afraid of his response, but she needed to know the truth.

"Ollie," she said. Her voice was quiet and

almost sad, "Are you embarrassed now to call me your friend?"

She looked up, straight into his eyes and found her answer.

"Oh, heck no," he lied. "We're still friends, but I need to tell ya' that I'm awful busy at the castle and well, I really won't have the time to come and visit you on a regular basis. It's not about your hair or anything. It's just that I have a real tight schedule and well . . . well . . . you're a smart girl. I'm sure you know what I mean."

"Yes," she said sadly, "I know exactly what you mean."

He felt like such a chump. He had rejected her in his own subtle way, breaking their bond of friendship as gently as he could. Even if the laws were changed to allow all colors of hair to live freely on this moon, he could never walk side-by-side with Priscilla, not now, not with her purple hair. Others might point fingers and laugh behind his back. They'd make fun not only of her but of him as well. He had his own image to think about, didn't he?

He tried to convince himself that his rejection

of her was a noble thing. It was best they go their separate ways.

"One day she'll thank me," he told himself, but in his heart he knew the real truth.

He was afraid.

Priscilla's back was now toward him. She had turned to face the night sky again, grateful for the darkness that now hid her tears. She felt her padded clothespin in her pocket. "A gift from a friend," he had said. With her whole heart she had believed him, but now, through no fault of her own, an overwhelming sadness filled her soul. She felt rejected and empty for she was once again, alone.

It was very quiet now on Ollie's balcony.

There was nothing more to say, nothing more to question. "I guess it's time to go home," Priscilla said.

She turned and faced Ollie, then gasped. For there in the black of the night she could see two peering green eyes. Ollie lifted the lantern. He heard the all too familiar evil chuckling of his one sworn enemy.

"Rodney!" Ollie whispered.

The devious cat waved Priscilla's bonnet that was now clutched in his right paw.

He chuckled again and then disappeared into the darkness.

26

Priscilla Alone

"Rodney, you little thief, bring that bonnet back," screamed Ollie, but the cat just snickered in the darkness.

"What's he saying?" Priscilla asked.

"He's saying, 'finders keepers.'"

"Are you sure that's what he's saying?" asked Priscilla growing more anxious by the second.

"I'm sure," responded Ollie. "I understand exactly what that infuriating, maddening, sneaky, night stalking cat is saying.

"So help me," Ollie screamed toward the stairs where Rodney had disappeared. "You bring that bonnet back or I'm coming after it myself."

"Meow, meow," the taunting cat chuckled again.

Ollie seethed. He felt himself losing his temper.

"What did he say this time?" asked Priscilla again.

"He said I must find him first and even if I do, he guarantees that I'll never catch him."

"Oh yeah, well, we'll just see about that," Ollie yelled back.

"That blasted cat," Ollie complained to Priscilla. "He's like salt poured into your deepest, sorest wound. He's like soap in your eyes. He's like a dentist drilling in your mouth on an open nerve without numbing your tooth up. He's like swallowing a whole mouthful of sea water. *He's the most irritating, teasing, exacerbating, annoying, drives-me-crazy-kind-of-cat I know!*"

"Ollie," Priscilla said, grabbing the blue baboon's shoulders. "Get a grip! I must have my bonnet back! You're my only hope!"

He looked deep into her big green eyes. He started to shake. Beads of sweat dripped from his blue-haired face. He remembered the fear he had felt just that morning, and then he suddenly realized the magnitude of their situation.

Ollie started to scream, but Priscilla was ready

for his reaction. She covered his mouth, and in a frightened but calm voice said, "Get my bonnet!"

He calmly nodded yes, but Priscilla waited a few seconds longer before removing her hand from his mouth. When she felt his hysteria was under control, she repeated again, "My bonnet, Ollie, you must get my bonnet."

His eyes were big as saucers. "I'm on my way," he said passing the lantern to Priscilla.

"But your torch has burned itself out," she cried. "How will you find Rodney with no light?"

"Don't worry. I'll find him." Ollie said with a determined tone. "If it's the last thing I ever do, I'll find that pesky cat and bring your bonnet back, too."

"And how do I get home?" she asked him.

"Meet me by the overhanging branch on the fourth floor," he yelled back. And with that he was gone.

"What am I to do?" Priscilla yelled down the black stairway. "And what about your plan to get me out of here? I want to go home," she called to the night. But all was silent. She heard no answer.

Warm tears began spilling off her cheeks. She thought about her father. He was here in the castle.

181

"Maybe, I should go to him," she pondered but then thought better of it.

"No!" she told herself. "It would only put him in grave danger."

She stood alone searching the night sky. "There had to be a way to safely maneuver to the fourth floor balcony, but how?" she questioned. Then she got an idea, an awful yet wonderful kind of idea.

"Yes," Priscilla said, smiling in the dark. "It just might work." And she felt a renewed strength and a strange, revitalized sense of courage that came from somewhere deep within. Her mind was clear.

She lifted the lantern then started down the tower stairs to the pantry door. She retraced her steps through the kitchens and then found her way to the first floor hallway where she could hear the king's loud voices still bickering.

Sensing Ollie's presence, she stopped briefly and then hurried on her way, intent on her mission. Priscilla quickly made her way to the stairwell where she began to climb. She passed by the second floor and laughed to herself when she remembered Ollie's attempt to pose like the kings.

He was a funny baboon. She would miss his sense of humor.

Priscilla moved more slowly as the stairway grew darker. The lantern was growing dimmer. There was no time to waste.

She now faced the large oak door that opened to the horrid third floor. She recalled how well they had worked together, her and Ollie, fending off those nasty rodents, but now she would go it alone.

She took a deep breath and pushed with all her might on the oak door. Hundreds of rats swarmed once again, curious about their intruder. Her loathing of these rodents nearly caused her to turn back.

"Turn back to where?" Priscilla thought. "No, this was the only way."

She walked to the center of the old ballroom and stood in the midst of them. The dim light revealed a multitude of rats itching for someplace to go. She needed the attention of these horrid creatures, so she stooped down and firmly grabbed the long tail of a very large rat. "It was successful once," she told herself. "It could be successful again."

She took a deep breath, circled the stunned

rodent high above her head, then started to run. The rats went into a frenzy.

"Follow me you wretched vermin!" she screamed. "You're about to make my day."

27

Rodney

Ollie followed Rodney, lickity split, down the tower stairs, through the pantry door and out into the hallway. Both royal pets knew the exact layout of the castle, "But where would that pesky cat hide?" wondered Ollie.

The blue baboon decided to formulate a new tactic in this serious game of Hide-And-Go-Seek. "I must gain the advantage," Ollie thought, "while providing an element of surprise." He began by hiding in the darkness, away from the flickering wall candles. He slowly climbed, using his tail to maneuver himself to the highest ceiling rafter located in the east end. It made for a good hiding place and allowed him to view the long, dimly lit hallway.

Ollie knew from experience that Norman's little pet was a very impatient cat. If he waited long enough, Rodney would reveal himself. And when he did, Ollie vowed to be ready.

The blue baboon waited, hidden in the dark rafter. He saw Priscilla pass by on her way to the fourth floor. He worried about her knowing the fear she must be feeling.

"Poor kid," he thought. She really was a brave girl, and though she could take care of herself, he still felt responsible for her safety. Darn that old Rodney anyway. He would have to mess things up.

It was getting late. The kings were winding down. Soon they would exit the great chamber and begin work on their *Special Project*. Paint cans and brushes lined the hallway. All was ready. The night was far from over.

Ollie was growing impatient as he realized that time was now a factor. He had to get that bonnet, and he had to get it soon. He wrapped his tail along the rafter ready to come out of hiding, but just as he was about to swing into the open he heard the sound of a rolling can of paint. He looked down the hallway and saw Rodney tiptoe-ing toward him. The notorious cat had Priscilla's bonnet on top of his head, the ties dangling on either side of his face.

Ollie nearly laughed out loud at the sight of him but kept control. He didn't want to blow his cover, for he definitely had the advantage.

Slowly and deliberately Rodney advanced, hiding occasionally in the shadowed walls.

"A little farther," Ollie thought. "Just a couple more steps and you're mine."

The instinctive cat slowly advanced then stopped. He now stood directly under Ollie's rafter. Rodney looked all around except up. He sniffed the air. He smelled the presence of his foe, but where was he?

Then out of the quiet came a snickering voice from above. "Here kitty, kitty."

Rodney lifted his head. Ollie was upon him.

28

Feast on That

Priscilla, with her lantern in one hand and her doomed rat in the other, fumbled to open the door leading to the fourth floor. Hundreds of crazed rodents, in anticipation of yet another dead carcass, followed her up the stairwell and to the door where they all waited. Delay of entry caused the squealing, crazed rats to gather at Priscilla's feet. They clawed at her ankles and wrapped their long tails around her lower legs. The feel of their coarse hair and wet tongues almost forced Priscilla to run in the opposite direction. But when the latch gave way she once again focused on the task at hand.

High in the rafters, Priscilla could hear the flapping of wings. She ran to the center of the fourth floor, twirling her hissing rodent as she went. When she felt sure the stampede had fully entered, she gave one final heave, hurling the doomed rat across the floor where other rodents swarmed, eating it alive. Little did they know that they were about to encounter the same fate.

With the rats' attention now diverted, Priscilla raced back to close the door again. There would be no escape.

Luckily, the bats were of the carnivorous type. They showed no interest in Priscilla. They swooped and swooshed and buzzed, capturing their unexpected treats before gliding to the rafters where they ate till their stomachs bloated with fresh meat.

Priscilla cringed at the sound of munching bats and squealing rats, but at least her plan had worked. The rest was up to Ollie.

She waited anxiously by the tree branch that overhung the fourth floor. "Where is he?" she wondered. "It's getting extremely late."

At last she heard the oak door open and the familiar, panicked voice of Ollie. "To the tree! To the tree!" he screamed.

She held the lantern high to see the blue-haired baboon racing in, her bonnet in his hand.

"Hurry, Ollie, hurry," Priscilla yelled back for she could see another creature coming into view.

"Rodney!" she gasped. He was closing in.

"To the tree!" Ollie screamed again.

She did as he ordered and crawled into the leafy arms of the tree while watching Ollie's tail grip a solid branch just above her.

Rodney, determined to get even, leapt in the same direction, but with no tail that gripped, he fell several feet below Priscilla. She looked and then gasped, for she could see the fearful cat dangling from a small, weak branch.

She remembered her own panic from the morning before when she hung from the mighty oak. It seemed so long ago. Now Rodney was in the same life-threatening position, and she knew that she could never leave without attempting to save him even if he was a mean, old cat.

"Get on my back," Ollie ordered Priscilla while handing back her bonnet. "We've gotta get out of here and now! The kings and their servants are all awake and making their way up the stairs. They heard Rodney screech and decided to follow him.

Hurry now, hurry! There's no time to lose." His voice was urgent.

Priscilla secured her bonnet in record time but sat in the tree refusing to leave.

"Meow, Meow!" Rodney's voice was pleading.

"We can't leave him," Priscilla said firmly. "He faces certain death if he falls. We must try and save him."

"Are you crazy?" Ollie couldn't believe what he was hearing. "Your dad and everyone else are coming up those stairs."

He then yelled down to the terrified cat below.

"Hey Rodney, now would be a great time to use one of those nine lives all you felines claim to have. Wish we could stay, but we gotta get going. See ya' later, sucker!"

"Oliver Matthew Molinka," Priscilla scolded, "I'm ashamed of you. Can't you see he's afraid?"

"Are you nuts?" Ollie was amazed at her lack of clear thinking. "You're in great danger, girl, real danger with that purple hair of yours. I've got to get you out of here and now!"

"I said I won't leave him, and I won't." Priscilla sat firm.

Ollie groaned with frustration. He gritted his teeth.

"Are you going to help him or not?" Priscilla asked.

"Why should I?" the blue baboon snapped back.

"Because it's the right thing to do," she simply stated.

"Oh! All right, then!" He knew there was no changing her mind.

He made his way down the tree, talking to himself as he got into position to save Rodney.

"I can't believe the messes I get into," he mumbled. "I might as well start my own business. I'll call it *Save Lives for Free, Inc.*"

"Hurry," Priscilla said.

"Get behind me," Ollie ordered. His tone reflected his irritation. "Now take my hand."

"A chain!" exclaimed Priscilla. "What a great idea! We can save him if we work together."

But her hopes were soon dashed when Ollie's hand lost her grip. He slipped and was left hanging upside down not too far from Rodney.

"Don't look down," Ollie instructed the petrified cat.

The blue baboon's tail was the only thing holding him to a leafy branch. He began to sway, arms out-stretched, reaching for Rodney, his enemy.

"On the count of three take hold of my hands, and I'll swing you to my back, Ollie ordered. "Just hang on, and I'll do the rest."

The royal cat was terrified. He shook his head no.

"Don't you shake your head at me," Ollie said angrily. "Do as I say or so help me, I will personally strangle you when this is all over."

Rodney's eyes grew wider. His branch was breaking. It was now or never.

Ollie began his count: "One, two, three. *Now!*"

The humbled cat closed his eyes. He felt the strong grip of the blue baboon. Then, scared and shaken, Rodney dismounted and moved to a stronger, more secure branch. Priscilla, still holding the lantern in one hand, swiftly blew out its dim light and positioned it behind her back. The stars were their only source of light now. No one made a move till the sound of other voices filled the air.

Then, without warning, the royal cat leapt back to the fourth floor balcony. Ollie groaned.

"We're doomed," he thought, for Rodney would surely lead the kings and their servants straight to the leafy branches where he and Priscilla hid in the darkness. He prepared for the worst as his eyes followed Rodney's every move.

Priscilla, however, saw something different in the royal cat's face. He had a mysterious look about him as if he were caught between two forces of equal power.

"This is Rodney's moment of truth," she thought. "He's come to a major crossroad in his life. The choice is his and his alone."

The now seemingly confused cat glanced in the direction of the kings and then back toward the tree where his rescuers waited. His eyes were peering at the branches as if searching for an answer, and then the old cat did a most unusual thing. He smiled, and with a slight nod of his head to the tree, he turned and charged his king.

Rodney's familiar, taunting chuckle echoed off the stone walls as he pounced on the red king's chest knocking him to the cold, hard floor. He began licking Norman's face in what Ollie and Priscilla knew was a staged distraction.

There was great commotion.

Norman shouted, "Get off of me you pesky cat." But Rodney persisted. He laid on Norman's chest and patted his majesty's hair, occasionally wrapping red curls around his clawed paws. Wynthor smirked then cheered at the red king's takedown while the rest of those gathered were engrossed by the cat's strange behavior.

Except for Albert.

Priscilla could see her father approaching the edge of the balcony. Thankfully she had placed the lantern behind her. He looked into the darkness toward the tree where she and Ollie sat frozen.

"Are my eyes playing tricks on me?" Priscilla's father wondered in the moon light.

He thought he saw something hidden in the tree: something yellow and something blue.

"No. Impossible," he silently told himself. He rubbed his eyes and looked again leaning a little closer as he did so.

"What are you looking at?" Wynthor yelled in Albert's ear, startling his blue-haired servant.

Albert put his arm around the shoulders of his

king, turning him away from the tree with its overhanging branches.

"Why nothing at all, Your Majesty," Albert said leading him away. "Nothing at all."

"Say," questioned Wynthor while stopping abruptly, "where's my blue baboon?"

"Oh, he wasn't feeling well this evening," Albert lied. "I put him to bed early. I'm sure he'll feel better in the morning."

"Well see that he does," Wynthor barked. "I'm holding you personally responsible. You and the rest of my cohorts, including the blue baboon, will publicly pledge allegiance to me. We will separate the blue-hairs from those inferior reds once and for all. Attendance is of the utmost importance. You will report to me, each and every one of you, or face a royal punishment. Now come along. We have work to do."

The kings began shouting orders once again. Then, precisely at the same moment, both Wynthor and Norman passed the loudest, most rank of all toots. It was a sound and a smell that startled even the munching bats who began to pelt their intruders with remains of half-eaten rodents.

"Let's get out of here," the kings screamed. Everyone ran except for Albert who turned to look at the branches one last time, but the leaves were now still, the colors gone.

29

The Long
Ride Home

Ollie glided through the trees with the greatest of ease. His tail gripped all the right branches which made for a smooth ride. Priscilla clung to his back, anxious to get home.

The trip to the castle had been filled with laughter and anticipation, but now there was a dark, awkward silence between them. There were no playful thumps of his tail, no dancing, no singing and no laughter. The truth was painfully clear: Fear and lack of courage does allow the madness to go on.

Priscilla tried to think of something to say but found herself at a loss for words. Besides, she knew that if she spoke, she would cry.

He maneuvered her back to their starting point. The giant oak stood strong and waiting. She endured the silence a few moments longer before starting her downward climb, hoping he would reaffirm their friendship in some way, but those moments were met with silence. She glimpsed at his eyes one last time. They appeared sad and tearful, glistening in the moonlight.

Each step, it seemed, put greater distance between them.

She finally stood on the forest floor looking up to where Ollie waited in the tree.

"It's been quite a night," Ollie laughed nervously, his voice cracking. He saw her face, then turned away. She looked so sad, as if she had just lost her best friend. And indeed she had.

"Well, I'll see ya' around," Ollie called to her. "Who knows," he continued, "one day we may meet up again."

And then he was gone.

"One day never seemed so far away," Priscilla whispered.

She began her walk home, still holding Ollie's

lantern. The brilliant prisms of light that had once filled the night sky were long gone.

"How symbolic," she thought as she trudged through the woods, then into the clearing. She suddenly felt very tired.

Priscilla thought of her father. His night was just beginning. It made her sad to think of him. He had come so close to discovering her. In a way, she wished he had.

After what seemed like a long time, Priscilla stood at her cottage door. She bent down, located the key and let herself in.

It was good to be home in familiar surroundings.

Then out of the darkness came her mother's, whispered voice. She sounded afraid.

"Priscilla, is that you?"

The young daughter, with tears now flowing, reached with outstretched arms and fell into the loving embrace of her caring mother.

30

True Confession

Never had Willa been so relieved in all her life. Her imagination, prior to Priscilla's return, had run wild. So, like any caring mother, she bombarded her daughter with questions and reprimands. But as she held Priscilla's tear-streaked face, she quickly realized that now was not the time to get hysterical. Now was the time to listen.

Priscilla knelt on the floor at her mother's feet. She was sorry for the worry she had caused, for her disobedience and deceit. She poured her heart out, telling her mother everything. She relayed not only the unbelievable chain of events of the last day and night but also her feelings of deep loneliness and her need to experience a true freedom of heart and mind. Priscilla talked of her father and what she had witnessed and felt just an hour ago.

Willa listened attentively without interruption to all that her daughter conveyed. She did not approve of Priscilla's disobedience but understood the why of it.

It was a long while before Priscilla's tears dried, her story completed. She slept now, exhausted, her head lying in her mother's lap. Willa gently stroked her daughter's hair with a loving and forgiving hand and with each gentle stroke, quiet tears of her own silently fell.

She thought of many things.

Priscilla was her pride and joy. There was nothing she wouldn't do for her daughter, and yet, Willa felt as if she had failed her in many ways. This life of isolation had taken its toll on all of them but especially her innocent child.

It was a long time before she helped Priscilla to bed.

She herself laid awake in anticipation of a new day. She wasn't sure where fate would lead, but she knew she could no longer stay hidden.

"Our '*One Day*' at last has come," she told her

sleeping Priscilla, "and should it present itself by way of storm with flashing streaks of lightning and roaring claps of thunder, then so be it. For I am no longer afraid."

Part Four

Then,

Both kings in their anger drew lines in the sand

Two lines that divided not only the land

But also the hearts and the minds of those there

Whose heads were all covered with red or blue hair.

31

Lines in the Sand

Albert woke with his body curled up on the royal platform. His mind had finally given into a few short minutes of sleep but not before finishing the blue line that officially separated the thrones of the two kings. A red line, drawn with the same intent next to the blue, finished the *Special Project*. The lines in the sand extended as far as the eye could see, circling the entire moon. The great division was now complete.

Albert yawned then stretched. Every bone in his body ached. The kings had long ago retired to their chambers leaving the work to their servants and others whom they had secretly paid to assist them.

Albert wanted nothing more than to crawl into his own bed and let the welcome gift of sleep wash over him, but that was impossible. This was a big day for their royal majesties. Both kings had great plans and long agendas. They would celebrate their official division by giving long and boring speeches filled with name calling and false information.

Albert had partial knowledge of Wynthor's plan. The blue-haired king would demand a public oath of allegiance from each of his servants. He would expect Albert to go first but Wynthor had failed to recognize one very important fact about his senior servant; Albert had grown tired.

He was tired of following orders that went against his values. He was tired of feeling ashamed. He was tired of hiding his wife and daughter. He was tired of his own lack of courage and the madness that surrounded him. Albert thought of his own despair from yesterday, the tears that overwhelmed him, the fear that had consumed him. He weighed all these things in his mind and then came to a final decision; he would take a stand.

No longer would he sit by in idle silence. Never would he pledge loyalty to a king like Wynthor or any other ruler who promoted hateful divisions, as symbolized by these lines in the sand.

He thought of Reverend Thomas Tooker, who so long ago had stood alone. Albert knew that he, like the Reverend Tooker, would pay dearly for his act of defiance, but his mind was set. If a free conscience meant his own banishment, then so be it. He had come to a major fork in the road of his life, and he would not retreat from what he believed was the right path.

He felt new hope.

He felt new courage.

He felt a new sense of quiet peace for he knew this day was his day of self-redemption.

32

To the Square

Priscilla woke to loudspeakers broadcasting the following command:

> "Hear ye, hear ye, hear ye. By order of their majesties, Kings Norman and Wynthor, all citizens who inhabit this moon, including the very young and the very old, must report to the castle square today by 10 a.m. Failure to do so will be considered an act of treason resulting in the gravest and harshest of consequences."

Priscilla's hair was wild as she entered the kitchen half-awake, looking for a quick breakfast. She fixed a bowl of cereal and poured herself a glass of juice. Her mother, she assumed, was still sleeping, for neither of them had gone to bed until the wee hours of the morning.

Priscilla recalled the previous evening and wondered if she had experienced nothing more than a bad dream. But when she noticed Ollie's nose closer lying on the table, she knew the events that she remembered had indeed transpired leaving her with many concerns.

Priscilla worried about her father. His physical exhaustion combined with his inner struggle made for a heavy burden.

"*One Day,*" he had promised, "things will change."

"Is this the day?" Priscilla wondered

She thought of Rodney and Ollie. "What would this day hold for them?" They would need a friend, Ollie, most of all, and though he had rejected her, Priscilla felt a strong bond still existed between them.

She thought about her mother who had listened so attentively to her story. Priscilla was grateful for her understanding.

She contemplated her life and the lives of those she cared about, and suddenly it was very clear.

Priscilla rose from the table pushing her breakfast aside. She was no longer hungry, no longer sleepy and no longer afraid. An inner voice was calling her. She knew where she must go and so she listened more intently to the kings' demands still blaring. They were ordering all citizens to report to the square. "Well I'm a citizen, aren't I?" Priscilla said out loud. "I'm entitled to the same rights as anyone else. But how do I convince my mother, that's my real challenge."

She paced the cottage floor, her mind in deep thought. It would not be easy to persuade her.

Priscilla heard the bedroom door open. She was surprised to see her mom all dressed in her very best and ready to go. Her anniversary comb was nestled in her soft, red curls. Her jaw was set, her eyes bright. She wore a look of unwavering determination.

"Where are you going?" Priscilla asked, though she knew the answer.

"Never mind," replied Willa as she closed her purse with a snap.

"I'm coming with you," Priscilla firmly replied.

Willa looked at her daughter with fiery eyes,

"No!' she said emphatically. "Your father forbids it, and so do I. It's too dangerous. I'd never forgive myself if they took you away. You must promise me that you will remain here where it's safe."

Albert had also forbidden Willa to come, but she did not reveal that part of her husband's order.

"Your father needs me." Willa's voice cracked with emotion. "I can't bear to think of him alone, and though I have no idea what this day will bring I do know that as his wife I must stand at his side."

"And as a daughter, I must stand by each of you. We are a family," Priscilla pleaded. "We must support one another. Please don't shut me out."

And then Priscilla repeated the same words she had confided to Ollie the night before, "I want a chance to be me," she said to her mother.

Willa looked deep into her daughter's eyes. Albert had forbidden the two of them to go anywhere near the castle. Yet, Priscilla's words rang true. They were a family, a proud family, and Willa's special sense of meaningful purpose for her daughter had never been stronger.

Then, out of the blue, Willa remembered words

of wisdom spoken long ago. They were the words
of Reverend Thomas T. Tooker:

*"Sometimes there is no right or wrong answer.
Sometimes there is only the burden of making a
difficult choice."*

The burden was hers. The choice was now.

She carefully weighed her daughter's words
and then knew in her heart what she must do.

"Get ready," she ordered Priscilla. "Put on your
best dress. We're going to the castle square."

33

The Mysterious Morning Mist

The early morning mist was an everyday occurrence. It covered the moon's surface for a brief time
at the beginning of each new day and was fully
absorbed by blue skies shortly after dawn. Priscilla
rarely paid any mind to this simple, daily event,
until today.

She didn't notice the mist at first. She was too
preoccupied with her own recollections of the last
twenty-four hours. She had experienced heart-
wrenching lows and amazing, uplifting highs.
Priscilla believed each happening, good or bad, had
brought her to this moment of joyful respect. The
bond that now existed between her and her mother

would bind them forever. It was a good feeling and one that she savored as they walked together across the clearing and onto the wooded path.

It wasn't long before Priscilla and Willa began to sense a strange aura in the forest. The morning mist, which normally would have faded by now, instead swirled and danced around the feet of the two travelers. It formed odd but friendly faces, spinning and dodging in a playful, care free manner. And though this activity appeared harmless, it left them both with an uneasy feeling, for the twirling mist seemed to have a life all its own.

Priscilla and Willa trudged onward, hoping the cloudlike vapors comprising the mist would evaporate. But the cool, foggy haze only intensified. Its movements became more aggressive. It churned higher, up to their waist lines and at times nearly covered Priscilla all together. The entire atmosphere seemed electrically charged, and the faces now formed by the rolling mist were faces that only Priscilla could identify.

She saw sad and fearful images of her father, of Ollie and of Rodney which frightened her, but when the churning mist outlined the blackness of

Wynthor and Normans' hate-filled souls, Priscilla froze. She was confused for the mist seemed to hold a paralyzing power. Was it good or was it evil? She stopped in her tracks, afraid to go on. Willa listened patiently to her daughter's frightening descriptions, and though she could not see what Priscilla now saw, she believed her all the same.

But it would take more than a morning mist to shake the mind set of Willa McDoodleNut-DoodleMcMae.

Retreat was not an option.

She took her daughter's hand, pulled her close and gave her a reassuring smile. "We must trust what we do not understand," Willa told her daughter. "Together, we can do anything."

And so they walked on, driven by an inner force they could not explain, motivated by a purpose not yet revealed, and confused by a mysterious mist that was now rolling, turning, rising up and then spiraling downward as if trying to convey a very important message. It filtered through the remaining trees of the forest allowing Priscilla and Willa to emerge easily from the wood without notice. They blended in with other moon travelers, anxious to reach their destination.

Willa's heart raced from anticipation of what lay ahead. She could see the newly painted red and blue lines through the gray mist. They extended outside the castle gate for miles and miles. The scene left her with a sick feeling, for she knew the horrible division, as symbolized by the lines in the sand, was now official.

The mist swirled over the painted lines like the shadow of a large, slithering, venomous snake ready to strike. It slowly crept along the entire sandy floor of the castle square, the crowd oblivious to its quiet presence. Only the watchful eye of one tall, yet gentle servant, standing on the platform noted it.

"What strange power is this?" Albert wondered.

"Is the churning mist good or evil?" he questioned. "Or is it just a fluke of nature? And what of the masses of people pressing steadily forward, their hostile feelings gaining in momentum like the mist that now encircles them?"

Albert feared for his fellow citizens. The impending storm he had felt for days was close at hand, and he was powerless to stop the fury it would surely render.

He began to despair, unaware that a small ray of hope now stood at the castle gate, a hope that would soon reveal itself through the courage of one lone voice and the unexplainable power of the swirling mist.

34

Where's Priscilla?

The crowd pressed ever closer; citizens from near and far poured through the open gate. The mist continued to swirl and churn around this multitude but few showed little, if any, interest in this rare phenomenon. They were, instead, preoccupied with the formal establishment of their own respective red and blue turfs. Nothing, it seemed, could distract them from that.

Willa stood with her daughter at the castle entrance. The hateful influences of Norman and Wynthor were apparent everywhere. But a new concern was now developing. She could see what appeared to be two, appointed gatekeepers. They were checking in all citizens according to their names and individual records of birth. All information was listed in two, huge ledgers, one red and one blue. Each citizen, having completed the check-in process, was then directed by the appropriate gatekeeper to the red or blue side of the square.

Willa had not anticipated this check-in procedure. There would be no record of her child's name, no date of birth, no proof that her daughter even existed.

Priscilla could see the worry on her mother's face. There was trouble up ahead, and the young daughter was smart enough to know that she and her bonnet posed a huge threat, not only for herself, but for her mother as well.

"On what side do I belong?" she asked innocently, knowing that her mother wondered the same thing.

Willa gave no verbal response to her daughter's question. She simply smiled and gripped Priscilla's hand a little tighter.

"As a mother, I will need to rely on all my instincts to somehow get my daughter through this mess," thought Willa.

But she knew this would not be easy for they were bottled in, stuck in a mass of angry citizens with no way out. Willa watched the crowd carefully. She began to maneuver to the side of the red gatekeeper, hoping Priscilla would go unnoticed, but as they drew closer, Willa grew more doubtful for both sides were now looking at Priscilla with pointed fingers and turned up noses. Willa inched forward, her shoulders back, her head held high. She displayed an air of confidence. Then, when the red gatekeeper became preoccupied with another citizen, she slipped out of the crowded check-in lane and over to the red side taking Priscilla with her. Willa was about to breathe a sigh of relief until she saw the red-haired gatekeeper approach her daughter. He shoved Priscilla to the side of the blues while shouting, "No person wearing a bonnet can stand on the red side."

"Well, they can't stand over here either," yelled the blue keeper of the gate, and he shoved Priscilla hard, back across the lines.

"The bonnet comes off," shouted the red and the blue gatekeepers.

"The bonnet stays on," Willa said with firm defiance.

There was fire in her eyes as her motherly instincts now surged from within giving her strength and courage. Like a female tiger, Willa stood firmly braced, ready to pounce in order to protect her young. Her hands were clenched into two tight fists, her back toward Priscilla. She took one step forward, and stood nose to nose with the two brutes who dared to push her daughter.

"The bonnet stays on," she repeated in a controlled seething voice.

"What's the reason?" asked the two suspicious thugs.

"My daughter has an extremely contagious disease. It's called Infectious Cranial Scalpitis. It's a horrible condition," Willa lied. "The poor girl has hundreds of strange, pus-filled sores all over her scalp. Anyone touching her bonnet runs the risk of contaminating not only themselves but anyone standing within ten yards of the infected source. "So leave her alone!"

The crowd and gatekeepers, not wanting to take a chance on contacting the dreaded scalpitis, backed away and dispersed immediately.

"Can you at least tell me your names?" yelled the red-haired gatekeeper who now stood about twenty yards away from Willa.

But Willa pretended not to hear.

The two gatekeepers tried asking again but then threw up their hands in disgust. Neither wanted anything more to do with this wild-eyed mother and her head sore, infected daughter. They quickly returned to their business at hand, leaving the feisty, redheaded woman alone.

Willa took a deep breath, relieved that her encounter had not developed into a full blown, physical confrontation. They were safe, at least for the present moment. But when she turned to take her daughter's hand, Willa gasped. Priscilla had vanished.

She looked frantically among the bickering citizens that now filled the square. Filled with desperation and gut-wrenching panic, Willa began pleading with those around her.

"Please," she cried, "my daughter, I can't find my daughter."

But no one heeded Willa's call. No one reached out to help. No one cared enough to think of someone else in need.

She looked toward the gatekeepers. They were

now smirking and pointing at the redhead who dared to challenge them just a few seconds ago.

She begged them, "Please, can you tell me which direction my daughter went?"

"We can't hear you." They chuckled, taking great pleasure in her pain.

"Please," she implored them once again.

"We haven't a clue, lady. So beat it! We have no further time for the likes of you."

Willa now felt the push of the crowd forcing her ever closer to the platform where Albert stood with Ollie and the rest of the servants.

She could see her husband's eyes overlooking the chaotic scene. She longed to call his name, to stand near him, for he was their devoted protector. But that was impossible for they were on opposite sides of the red and blue lines and that made them enemies according to the kings' law.

Albert observed the pandemonium below him. The madness had reached a new height. Like a slow-moving, motion picture show, the scene unfolded before him. Yet amid all the distraction, Albert was able to feel a special presence. Willa was very near, of that he was certain. His head turned to the exact spot where she now stood. He rubbed his eyes not once, not twice, but three times hoping that what he saw was only an illusion. He did not want her exposed to the mayhem that was now taking place.

Slowly, the truth began to wash over him. He began to tremble for there was no mistaking her; the woman he saw standing in the square was indeed his wife. Albert observed her frantic behavior. She was fighting her way through the crowd and turning her head in every direction as if looking for someone, but whom?

And then the unthinkable came to his mind. "Was it possible that Priscilla was lost in the chaos below?"

Albert looked at his wife, afraid of what he suspected but desperate to know the answer. She could feel his penetrating gaze, and when her eyes looked up and locked with his, he knew the painful truth.

Hot tears streamed from Willa's tired eyes down her anguished face. "Would he ever forgive her for bringing their daughter to this place? "Would she ever forgive herself?" She turned away, not wanting to see his pain, his torment.

She held her head, feeling suddenly dizzy as if she were floating on a wave in a sea of raging waters. She could feel herself reaching in the darkness, desperate to find the hand of her lost daughter whose fate, it seemed, was now controlled by an outgoing tide. How far would this tide of angry faces and hateful eyes take her? Would she return unharmed? All seemed dark now. There was no sign of her dear Priscilla.

And then . . .

35

Discovery

Like a miracle, there appeared on the side of the blue, a familiar face. It was old Mr. Zotter, the quiet clock maker. He had made his way to the edge of the blue line and now stood directly across from Willa.

"Can you help me?" she pleaded. "I'm desperate. "Please, I need a friend, someone I can trust, someone who will keep my most precious secret safe. I've lost my daughter, and I feel so helpless." Willa put her face in her hands. She wanted someone, anyone, to tell her that Priscilla was safe.

Old Mr. Zotter smiled and then spoke in a soft and caring voice, "My dear," he said, "I know how frightened you are, and mind you, I understand more than what you think. But you must not give into despair for I have learned that often times the most heart-breaking moments are the ones that lead us to where we were meant to go in the first place."

"My daughter is lost," Willa confided again to Mr. Zotter. "She's lost and all alone. I'm not sure what to do or where to go."

As she spoke her tears began to fall again. She scanned the crowd with frantic eyes but to no avail.

Mr. Zotter stepped closer to the edge of the blue line. He motioned for her to do the same from the red side.

She obliged him but couldn't help wondering what the old man was up to. He was acting somewhat strangely, Willa thought. He wore a long, black, oversized, cloak that seemed to bulge on his right side. There was a twinkle in his eye and a look of mischief in his smile.

He leaned forward.

"I have something to show you, Willa," the old clock maker said. "It is something that I believe will help ease your troubled mind. But first you must promise that you will not react to what you're about to see, for any outburst would greatly endanger my surprise. Do you promise?"

Willa had no idea why Mr. Zotter would make

such a strange request or why he was wearing such a long outer garment on this warm, summer day, but she decided to play along. "I promise," she said. And though her heart and mind were elsewhere, she managed now to focus on her friend. She was curious as to what kind of surprise he had in store.

He looked cautiously to his left and then to his right. Everyone around them was busy arguing. Not a single soul paid the slightest attention to the old man now facing the tearful redhead.

"I do believe my dear lady," the clock maker said with a smile, "that what you're looking for is right here."

With that he carefully opened his cloak ever so slightly.

Willa gasped, then quickly put her hand to her mouth for fear of crying out her feelings of joy and relief. There in the confines of the old man's garment, stood Priscilla. She gave a small wave then whispered in her softest voice, "Hi Mom," before Mr. Zotter quickly covered her again.

"But, how did you know?" Willa's mind was racing with ten-thousand questions. "How did you know that she was my child?"

"That part was easy," Mr. Zotter replied. "She has your loving eyes.

"I know you have many questions, my dear, but I can answer only a few for the mist is rising. Soon it will envelop the entire square, and we must stand ready to embrace its purpose. You will receive the answers to your questions later," he continued. "In the meantime I will keep your daughter with me till it is safe for you to rescue her. No harm shall come to her for as you can see, little attention is given to the old."

Willa knew he was right but still frowned at the thought of surrendering her daughter again.

"Where will you take her?" Willa asked for she was still very much concerned for Priscilla's safety. Mr. Zotter seemed to read her mind.

"There is a small, hidden stairway located at the back of the platform. It leads to a secret hiding place below," the old man explained. "I will take Priscilla there. She will remain safe for the hidden stairs can serve as a way in or a way out. Your husband is aware of these secret stairs, therefore, no harm shall come to Priscilla for Albert will be close at hand."

"But how will you safely maneuver Priscilla to this hiding place?" Willa asked, still afraid.

Mr. Zotter smiled a patient smile.

"We will climb the royal staircase and then cross the platform to the stairs."

"In broad daylight?" Willa asked in a whisper that was full of panic. "But . . . but . . . but . . . " she stammered

The timepiece maker held up his hand to gently signal enough.

"Trust me, my lady."

He looked to his left and then to his right. No one paid any mind to the wise, old man. He smiled at Willa then pulled from a deep inside pocket, a black hood similar to the one hooked to his cloak. "Like this my dear," he said while demonstrating what she needed to do. Priscilla nodded her head and followed his lead, the two of them securing their hoods at the same time. In an instant Mr. Zotter and Priscilla vanished.

Willa was stunned. She looked up to the platform where her husband stood. His keen eyes had witnessed all that had transpired. He appeared calm as if he understood. His sweet Priscilla was safe for the moment, hidden in the confines of a gentleman's old, mystical cloak.

36

The Secret Identity of Old Mr. Zotter

It felt strange to climb the royal stairs and then walk across their majesties' platform without a single notice. Priscilla had felt afraid, but the hoods of Mr. Zotter had allowed them to pass safely. She descended now to her place of hiding guided by the old clock maker's hand. Together they removed their mysterious head coverings making them visible once again.

Priscilla thought of her father. It gave her comfort to know that he was near. She longed for his protective arms but knew she must wait patiently. And while she waited she did a quick survey of her surroundings.

The area was large enough for her and the slightly hunched over Mr. Zotter to stand comfortably. Two old logs partially buried in the sandy floor provided a place to sit. Strangely, the stairs they had just descended were no longer visible. It puzzled her. She had many questions. How long would she and her new companion sit here in this strange, protective place? When would they return to the square? Was there a special plan that Mr. Zotter needed to carry out? What of the disappearing staircase? And what was her purpose in all of this?

Priscilla was fairly certain that Mr. Zotter held the answers to her questions, and though she was anxious to learn more she decided to sit quietly. She would wait for him to break the silence.

Priscilla repositioned herself on the bumpy log, her chin in hand. She stared at her new protector who sat directly across from her.

"I don't believe I've properly introduced myself," Mr. Zotter said with a smile. "My name is Zachariah Zotter. Some call me the old clock maker. Some call me an old keeper of time and some just call me old."

Priscilla sat mute. He appeared to be a kind, old man, but she wasn't sure. She had been terribly afraid when he had whisked her into his overcoat with strict orders not to make a sound. She had listened obediently to his command mainly because she was too afraid to do anything else, but when he guided her to her mother, she had felt reasonably safe.

Still, he was technically a stranger, and so she held back any information about herself.

Feeling her hesitation, Mr. Zotter closed his eyes in pretended concentration. "Your name," he said, snapping his fingers, "is Matilda."

Priscilla shook her head no in response.

"How about Lottie?"

"No," she replied, now recognizing the old clock maker's game.

"Gladys?"

"Nope."

"Ninabelle?"

"Uh-uh."

"Annabelle?"

"Negative."

"How about plain old Belle?" he said, throwing

his hands in the air as if he were giving up on this impossible name game.

"No!" giggled Priscilla. "My name," she said proudly, extending her hand, "is Priscilla McDoodle-NutDoodleMcMae. I am very pleased to make your acquaintance, Mr. Zachariah Zotter, and I thank you for your rescue."

He smiled, clearly taken in by her charm.

"The pleasure and the honor is all mine," he said shaking her small hand and giving a slight bow of his head.

"I want you to know, Priscilla," he now spoke in a serious tone, "that I thought it most brave of you to try and lose yourself in the crowd the way you did in order to protect your mother. The gatekeepers were rather rough on you."

Priscilla was surprised. The old clock maker had witnessed her retreat and understood the reason for it. She studied his mysterious face. He appeared to know a great deal about many things.

"It was the only way to keep my mom safe," Priscilla simply stated. "The gatekeeper would have allowed her to stand on the red side but not with me. I had no place to go. I knew she'd never leave me, so I did the only thing I could do," Priscilla shrugged her shoulders. "I was afraid for her. It really was nothing. I did what anyone would have done."

He smiled at her innocence. "Never the less," he persisted, "it was still a very brave thing. I saw the whole incident from my little shop and decided to put on my long overcoat and venture out just in case you needed a friend."

"Friend," she said, her face suddenly sad. "I had a friend once."

The wise, old clock maker made no response. Instead he sat patiently and waited for her to continue.

Priscilla looked down. "It was my fault," she said. "You see there are flaws about me that my friend found difficult to handle."

Mr. Zotter felt Priscilla's pain of rejection. He noted that through it all, this brave little girl still displayed a forgiving nature and humble inner strength.

"She is clearly the chosen one," he thought. Her obvious virtues would empower her to speak for them all, if she chose to do so.

"Are you referring to your purple hair?" Mr. Zotter asked quite matter-of-factly.

Priscilla's mouth opened wide in total surprise but no sound was there. She immediately began fumbling with her bonnet thinking purple strands of hair had somehow slipped through.

"Relax, my dear," he told Priscilla, taking her hands and calmly placing them on her lap. "The truth is, I have known about you and your family for quite some time. You see," he continued, "my cousin is the Reverend Thomas T. Tooker. He secretly married your mother and father years ago. He and your father were the best of friends. They respected each other. Your father would often confide in Thomas and Thomas, before he was banished, confided in me. My cousin never broke your father's confidence but when Thomas was ordered off this moon, the good Reverend Tooker shared your family story with me. He gave me specific instructions to protect you and your family. Though you never knew him, you held a special place within my cousin's heart."

"But no one ever knew of my existence,"

Priscilla said, confused. "I've lived in isolation all my life."

"Thomas knew. You see your father would often speak of you and your gorgeous purple hair. He said you were beautiful on the inside as well as the outside. He was right."

Just then Priscilla and Mr. Zotter were startled by the racket from above. The two kings were screaming and stomping their feet. It felt as if the entire platform might cave in.

"Was the moon always like this?" Priscilla asked, looking up.

The keeper of time looked sad and far away.

"No, not always," he said. "Years ago this moon was a peaceful place where citizens accepted one another and embraced their differences. Their *Whys* were heard and respected for growth of spirit comes when we dare to question. People spoke with kind and caring voices, considerate of each other and always willing to lend a helping hand. It was a time of laughter, a time of joy, a time of harmony.

"It was wonderful," Mr. Zotter said with a soft smile.

He looked at Priscilla with intense eyes as he continued his story.

"My cousin and I came to this moon filled with hopes and dreams. All was peaceful for a time. And then Norman and Wynthor somehow came into power. Slowly the population changed their way of thinking. They were taken in by the selfish, unfeeling teachings of the kings."

The old man lowered his eyes and shook his head.

"Worst of all," he continued, "those who frowned on the kings' philosophy kept silent and as a result the moon became a very dangerous place to live.

"I remember the day Thomas was banished. He stood alone. I said nothing in his defense, and I've regretted that silence everyday since then. I have vowed never to stand silent again."

Priscilla listened, captivated by his story. Mr. Zotter, like her father, harbored deep regrets of that fateful day, and he, like her father, was a very good man.

The mysterious, old clock maker then stood and took Priscilla's hand.

"I will need to leave you very soon, my child, for I must take my place in the square, but before I go, there are a few things I must tell you."

Priscilla sensed his serious tone. She sat straight and tall on the old log, her green eyes glued to the face of this understanding, old man.

"The rising mist," he began, "with its strange and awesome power will soon paralyze every voice of every gathered citizen in the square including the two mighty kings. It will freeze everyone in their tracks for a short period of time. Their voices will go mute but their eyes and ears will remain open forcing them to listen to one special messenger who will dare to ask *Why?*

"The messenger will challenge all who are present to a new way of thinking. This will not be an easy task. It will take a special kind of strength from within."

"Who is this messenger?" Priscilla asked with growing excitement.

"Why, you of course," said Mr. Zotter, smiling.

Priscilla was stunned. "Me?" she said in disbelief. She stood and faced the old timekeeper.

"But it's against the law to question *Why?*" she said in a panicked voice.

"And besides," Priscilla continued, "I couldn't possibly stand in front of all those people. No!" she said shaking her head, "you must be mistaken."

"My dear child," he said patiently, "there is no mistake. "When you've lived as long as I have you will come to know and understand the meaning of Presence. I am fortunate, for I have heard this loving Presence speak to me on more than one occasion. This is just such an occasion. The message is clear. You have the power to make a difference. The choice is yours."

"But, I'm afraid," Priscilla's voice was barely a whisper.

"Search your heart," the wise, old man advised her. "You will know the moment, you will find the words and you will discover a special courage if you look deep within your own soul. You may even find that special friend again. But above all, dare to ask *Why?*"

He then rose from the old log. "I think you will find this useful," he said, and he handed back to Priscilla the hood of his cousin. He detected her fear and apprehension as she gazed at the mysterious head covering now resting in her hands.

"Be open to the Presence that surrounds you," he said fervently. "Listen to its voice for it will surely guide you down the right path that will lead you to your destiny."

He smiled then covered his head.

And with that, old Mr. Zotter was gone, leaving Priscilla to ponder all that he had told her.

37

A New Law

Both kings were growing more restless by the minute, anxious for their "royal" day to begin. Tensions were mounting, and as a result, their tooting began to escalate along with their obnoxious behavior.

"What time is it? What time is it?" Wynthor yelled over and over again while Norman kept looking at himself in his royal, hand-held mirror. "Fix this curl," he barked at his servants. "Fix it at once or face a severe punishment. I must look perfect."

The square was filled to capacity with angry citizens. The lines in the sand were having their desired effect as the two sides were in danger of growing into a dangerous mob, capable of anything.

Albert kept a close eye on Willa and then glanced at those present on the royal platform. All servants were in attendance including the blue baboon who was acting very odd. He seemed distant and wore a very sad look on his face. Each time Albert approached him, he would run in the opposite direction, clearly avoiding him. But why?

Norman's cat was behaving very strangely, too. Both pets kept eyeing each other as if they shared something of great importance. This caused Albert to question his observations from the night before. "What hidden figures had he sensed in the trees? Was it possible? Could it have been his own daughter and the blue baboon?" he wondered.

But now there were other pressing issues to worry about. The hostile crowd was growing more intense with each passing moment, and the fast swirling mist, which seemed to go unnoticed by its citizens, was moving with a stronger energy. Albert kept close watch for he sensed the moon was on the brink, but on the brink of what?

"The time," Wynthor barked, "the time."

Albert, startled back to the present moment, patiently answered his king. "I am aware of the time, Your Majesty. Everything is under control."

"Well see that it is and remember," the blue

haired king repeated for the tenth time this morning, "you will proclaim your allegiance at precisely 11 a.m. Do not fail me," he ordered. Then turning on his heel he tooted loudly before taking his place in the royal line.

Albert gave the signal for the trumpets to sound. It was 10 a.m. The crowd came to attention and now looked to their leaders with great anticipation. Each king quickly took his place on his individual throne. Both were eager to speak.

Which side would exhibit the greater strength? Which king would dominate in the end?

Norman stood first. He strutted silently for a minute or two, primping his hair with his left hand while clinging to his lapel with his right. He stopped in dramatic fashion and slowly pulled out a scroll from the right, inside sleeve of his jacket. He lifted the scroll and primped his hair one last time before unrolling the parchment. Then, with his nose in the air and a smirk on his face, he proceeded to read in a loud, drawn-out fashion his official written message.

"Uh, uh hem," Norman began by clearing his throat. "Beginning today," his red majesty roared.

"I'm here to enforce a new law that I wrote. That law reads as follows:

From this day forward,
'tis I . . . I, King Norman, who will reign
as sole ruler of this moon.
I shall be your one true leader. Therefore,
effective immediately,
my word IS LAW, and all must obey.
Furthermore,
since it is a known fact that redheads
are naturally wiser and smarter
than blue-haired people.
I, being the wisest of all,
further decree that all redheads,
and only redheads,
will have the privilege to speak their own minds
but only if their minds are in total
agreement with mine.
In short your voice will not count
if your hair is all blue.
Furthermore,
The word Why will continue to be a
nonexistent term in our vocabulary. Any use of

this word will be considered an act of treason,
punishable by the gravest of consequences.
For the moon will, without question,
be governed
by me, King Norman, for as long
as I shall live.

The redheads began cheering while the blues sat in protest. Norman waved his clutched hands high over each shoulder. He kept motioning to the crowd to cheer louder. Then after many minutes, he turned on his heel and waved the rolled up scroll in Wynthor's face.

"Deal with that, you ugly, old fool!" Norman said in a taunting voice. "Soon, I shall rule this moon alone, for I am mightier than you, and just in case you haven't looked in a mirror lately," taunted Norman some more, "anyone can see that I am, by far, much better looking than you."

He then laughed a sinister, uncontrollable laugh while pointing at the blue-haired king. The reds followed Norman's action and began laughing and pointing at the blues.

Albert feared a riot might break out. He

wished old Norman would stop his jeering to prevent such a possible outburst, but the red-haired king just gloated and laughed all the harder. He was extremely pleased with himself at the present moment, for he felt quite confident that no one, least of all Wynthor, could ever top his fine delivery of such an eloquent and powerful speech. He plopped his royal bottom on his royal, ruby throne and savored the moment.

The crowd grew quiet again.

It was Wynthor's turn to speak.

38

The Blues Have Their Say

The blue-haired king rose from his throne very slowly. His face seethed, and his body shook from a rare kind of fury. He stood and muttered to himself while pounding his clenched, right fist into his open left hand. He was like a ticking bomb ready to explode at any moment.

All eyes were upon him. Everyone waited in fearful anticipation as the blue-haired king paced back and forth on the royal platform.

Wynthor knew he must get control of his feelings. The power of his spoken words would depend upon a calm and effective voice, and though his written speech was rather short, he was determined to leave a lasting impression on all those present.

After what seemed like a very long time, Wynthor's pacing came to a stop. He now stood and faced the blue crowd with uplifted hands. His voice rang out with an evil, vengeful tone.

"Well," he said, imploring the blue-haired citizens with extended arms, "are we going to take this kind of abuse? No! I tell you! We are superior! Raise your fists! Down with the reds! Down with them all."

The blue-haired citizens rose and did as their king ordered. They faced the red-hairs with hateful looks.

"Stay on your own side," shouted the blues.

"Don't cross this line," the reds retorted.

"Blues are smarter than reds!"

"No!" The reds answered.

"Don't breathe our air," the blues demanded, waving their clenched fists.

"Don't touch one grain of our sand," the reds replied.

"Your sand is filled with cat manure!" The blue-hairs shouted.

"Oh yeah, well, your sand stinks from baboon droppings," the reds yelled back. "Take a whiff of this!"

The two groups began kicking sand into the faces and eyes of their opponents. Children observing their parents did the same. The moon was in a frenzy.

"This crowd needs to break up and go home," Albert implored his king but Wynthor wasn't finished. He would have his say. He turned his head and addressed Norman directly.

"You are a redheaded fool. Your brain, it's all jumbled inside of your head. 'Tis I who will lead! I am king, and I do hereby decree that you and every moon person will, from this day forward, answer to me."

Norman plugged his ears with his fingers. He watched in disgust as Wynthor walked to the edge of the platform and faced the crowd again, this time on bended knee. With hands folded, he lifted his eyes as if he were in deep meditation. He continued this way for a minute or two and then addressed the gathered mass again.

"The fates have spoken." Wynthor spoke firmly.

"The power to rule is mine and mine alone. All reds will obey my commands, including Norman. Anyone refusing to do as I say will suffer the gravest of consequences."

Wynthor then snapped his fingers and summoned his senior blue servant.

The eleventh hour was only a few minutes away.

Albert stepped forward.

"Stand here, next to me," the blue-haired king instructed him. "Now wave to the crowd," Wynthor ordered while smiling through gritted teeth. "Upon my command you will pledge your allegiance." He handed Albert a pre-written statement.

"This affidavit will cover everything you will need to say," Wynthor continued to instruct him. "Remember, this is your idea. You must sound convincing."

Albert quickly scanned the document. It was filled with fictitious stories of false heroic deeds. It lauded the "just ways" of the blue-haired king and praised him for his "wisdom and kind heart."

"I cannot read such a pledge," Albert simply said.

"You *can* and you *will*," His Royal Blue Majesty commanded.

The verbal war in the square was deafening and gave cause to delay. Fists on both sides were held high as citizens threatened one another, and all the while the mist kept rising in a most mysterious way. The moon was on the brink of disaster.

In the middle of it all stood Willa. She watched as Wynthor and Albert appeared to be in confrontation with one another. Was there no one who would stand with her husband in defiance of the corrupt kings? She looked to the platform and studied each face, her eyes coming to rest on the blue baboon.

"Ollie," Willa whispered to herself. She remembered Priscilla's description of her high-strung, blue-haired friend from the night before, and though she'd never met him, Willa felt as if she knew him.

She sensed his desire to do the right thing. She felt his inner battle, his wish for strength of mind, his prayer for heartfelt courage and his longing for one more chance at friendship.

The terrified baboon stood along the west edge

of the platform, his face in his hands, his backside now so close to the hidden stairs.

"Do not despair, my little friend," Willa whispered. "You are not alone for Priscilla waits in the shadows."

39

Ollie's Turmoil

Ollie stayed to the back of the platform, and though he knew every part of the castle, he was unaware of the hidden, secret stairs behind him. Only Albert and Mr. Zotter and now Willa knew of the mysterious passageway that led to the area below the thrones. It was a place that seemed to harbor strange, unnatural powers.

Priscilla began to pace back and forth contemplating Mr. Zotter's words. The rays of filtered light now revealed the hidden stairs, illuminating her way to the platform. The light, it seemed, was calling her. Slowly, she began her ascent. Not wanting to reveal herself just yet, she secured Reverend Tooker's hood over her yellow bonnet. She was now hidden from the naked eye.

Ollie had no idea that just behind him stood

his once best friend. He missed her company and, he deeply regretted his reaction to her purple hair. As a matter of fact, he had thought of nothing else since their parting a few short hours ago, and now, he had to admit, he had never felt so alone in all his life. He was miserable, and he had no one to blame but himself.

Priscilla climbed the final two stairs and stood slightly behind her friend. Ollie was just an arm's length away. She recognized his typical symptoms of fear. His whole body shook, and his blue hair was on end. He covered his eyes with his trembling hands in order to block out the chaotic scene before him.

"Yup," she said to herself. "It's Ollie all right."

He was embarrassed and ashamed. Guilt hung over him like a dark cloud. He avoided Albert's eyes for he had unjustly rejected his daughter's friend-ship. He had even made her cry. Worst of all, upon self-examination, Ollie had discovered in his own heart, one major truth about himself.

He was nothing more than a chicken, a scaredy cat, a yellow-bellied lowlife, plain and simple.

He had rejected Priscilla for selfish reasons. It

was *his* own image that had concerned him. It was *his* prejudice that had prevented him from recognizing Priscilla's inner gifts, and it was *his* own lack of courage that had left him feeling sad and alone.

It was time to change, he decided, and that change needed to start now. He uncovered his eyes, ready for any challenge. Or so he thought.

"I'm turning over a new leaf," he told himself with confidence. "My heroic side will from this moment on, dominate my chicken side. Every moon person shall recognize me as the new *Brave Heart.*

He was bursting with self-pride and a heart filled with good intentions. "I'll put a stop to all this red-and-blue hair nonsense," he continued. "I'll lead others to truth. I'll stand up for justice. I'll rescue those in need."

His mind was racing, but when his eyes came to rest on Albert who was now caught in the firm grip of Wynthor's strong right hand, he became terrified once more. He wondered if the new, heroic side of Oliver Matthew Molinka should speak up in Albert's defense. The mere thought of challenging the kings sent him into a panic. He could feel his chicken side dominating his *Brave Heart* side.

"If only Priscilla was here," he spoke to himself. "She would give me strength. She would help me make the right choice. I cannot save the moon alone!"

And then he felt an eerie presence. "Priscilla," he whispered. He looked around but saw no one.

"I must be losing my mind," Ollie thought.

Priscilla now stood at the top of the stairs. She made no sound. She watched as Wynthor grabbed more tightly the arm of her father, but no amount of pressure would shake Albert's commitment to the truth and what he felt was right. His jaw was set, his arms crossed in front of him. He stared straight ahead.

The clock was now chiming the eleventh hour.

"I command you to speak!" Wynthor's voice was desperate. He looked as if he wanted to do great bodily harm to his senior servant who dared to disobey him.

The crowd waited. A strange silence now filled the air while all eyes focused on Albert who continued to stand frozen in open defiance. The clock seemed deafening as it sounded its seventh chime, then eight, then nine.

The mist now rose and danced with wild abandon around the throng of red and blue citizens. The crowd at last took notice, and suddenly everyone was afraid.

Soon all would be rendered speechless.

All but one.

Wynthor looked around. His moment of glory was falling apart. He now grabbed the neck of Albert and raised his hand as if to strike him.

Priscilla's heart pounded. She feared for her father. The eleventh hour was at hand.

And then . . .

A single voice rang out for all to hear.

40

Chaos in the Square

"*Ouch!*" screamed Ollie.

Priscilla had pinched his butt hard causing him to jump several feet into the air. She felt bad for she knew her pinch had undoubtedly caused Ollie some pain, but his reaction had also drawn attention away from her father, at least for the time being, and for that she was grateful. Ollie looked back to where he had stood.

"A bee," he thought, "a giant, humongous, nasty, old bee must have stung my behind." But his eyes saw nothing to prove his theory correct.

The blue baboon's high pitched voice had caused all eyes, including Wynthor's, to fall on him.

"*You idiot!*" the blue-haired king yelled in outrage at the baboon. "Explain yourself."

"Well, uh . . . you see, Your Majesty, I have a

very sensitive rear end, and occasionally I get these spasms in my gluteus maximus which are quite painful. One never knows when one of these horrible spasms will occur." Ollie said while rubbing his behind. "I am sorry for the interruption, your majesty, truly I am. By the way am I bleeding?" Ollie asked, while sticking his rear end up to Wynthor's face for inspection.

The blue-haired king backed away in disgust. "Get your ugly rump out of here," he said. "Who cares whether you're bleeding or not, certainly not I. You are a worthless pet without a brain in your head. Don't you realize my historical moment was ruined because of you?

"You interrupted my senior servant's pledge, you twit. As a result, I can no longer keep you as my royal pet. You are incompetent and quite frankly, I don't even like you. Therefore, by the power vested in me, I hereby make the following decree:

No royal pets with sensitive rear ends
that are prone to spasms are allowed
on my moon.

"*Your* moon?" Norman yelled in disbelief. "This isn't your moon," he protested. "This is my moon!" And the same old confrontation started all over again.

The kings were screaming and tooting. The mist was churning and swirling, and the gathered citizens were now beginning to panic. Total bedlam ensued.

Then out of the shadows the silhouette of a small girl emerged. She stood at the center of the royal platform. A black hood lay at her feet.

Albert turned.

"Priscilla?" he whispered.

But his joy quickly turned to fear for the mist was now upon him. It froze him and all others both in the square and on the royal platform. The swirling haze had entered the nostrils of every individual. Its sweet, alluring scent was pleasant enough, but its paralyzing power caused great fear.

Wynthor ran to his throne seeking protection, but no human was spared. All stood frozen, unable to move their arms and legs. Their mouths were mute, yet, their eyes and ears remained alert.

Only one small girl was unaffected by the mist. She was the messenger.

Ollie stood in disbelief, overcome with joy and fear at the sight of his friend. Strangely, he and Rodney were unaffected by the mist, their animal nature somehow immune to its Presence. An eerie silence now filled the air. There was no choice. All would listen to Priscilla's words.

Everything had happened just the way old Mr. Zotter had said it would. The eyes of every individual now rested on the little girl standing center stage.

Priscilla took a deep breath then slowly walked to the front of the platform. She embraced her father though he could not return his own sign of affection. She looked into his tearful eyes and saw his fatherly love, his deep pride and his unmistakable fear.

Priscilla next looked down to the worried face of her mother who had longed for freedom not only for herself but for a daughter whom she loved and cherished more than life itself.

Then scanning the blues Priscilla spotted the

twinkling eyes of old Mr. Zotter. She sensed his wisdom, his confidence. He believed in her.

Priscilla glanced back at Ollie.

"Who knows," the old clock maker had said, "you may even find that special friend again."

She looked to Rodney who had saved her and Ollie the night before.

She saw the smugness, the hate and desire for power in the faces of Norman and Wynthor.

And suddenly her desire to speak for what was fair and just began to fill her mind and heart.

"One day," she had often said, "I would like a chance to be me."

She wondered if there were others who desired the same freedom, who longed for acceptance, and who, if given the chance, could make a difference in the lives of those they encountered along life's way. "Who would speak for them?" she wondered.

The air was thick with anticipation. Both kings now sat on their thrones, quiet for once, waiting for this small little girl to make her move.

She stood firmly planted, one foot extended over the red line and one foot over the blue, her mouth turned upward in a sweet, simple smile.

With a sense of pride Priscilla reached up and calmly removed her bonnet allowing her purple hair to flow around her face and down her shoulders. She felt an instant sense of freedom, the weight of her secret now lifted.

Some of her fellow citizens nearly fainted at what they saw. All were in shock, except for Willa who stood smiling with pride at the sight of her daughter's soft, purple curls.

Priscilla faced the two stunned kings. She curtsied before them. They began gasping for air, and their eyes nearly popped from their sockets at the sight of her. She observed their hearts thumping hard and fast through their royal, velvet coats. Both kings tried desperately to speak, but no words came. They blinked their eyes till they were sore hoping that she was only an illusion.

But Priscilla was not an illusion. She was real, and she needed the help of a friend now more than ever.

Ollie watched as the scene unfolded before him, and he suddenly knew his purpose. This was his moment of truth. With knees shaking, he went to Priscilla's side and gently took her hand.

"The purple looks great," he whispered. And those four simple words from that simple baboon gave strength to Priscilla to speak for the moon.

Part Five

And while they stood thinking, both kings from their thrones

Now studied Priscilla with moans and with groans.

They had no real answer, she asked them again

But this time the question was louder and then

A strange thing, it happened, the red and the blue

Now asked the same question and that's when she knew

Their moon could be saved if they only would try

And so with one voice, they together asked, "Why?"

41

Priscilla Speaks

This was the day. This was the hour. This was her moment.

"Be open to the Presence," Mr. Zotter had said.

Then heeding his words, Priscilla took a deep breath ready now to fulfill her destiny.

"Your Majesties, please," she looked up to the sky.
"I have just one question. My question is Why?
Why?" asked Priscilla, *"do eyes fail to see*
The good that is present in you and in me?
For though we are different, we still are the same.
We cry and we laugh and we each have a name.
And all these good people, the RED and the BLUE
Should have the same rights as your majesties do
Including the freedom to live without fear
At peace with our neighbors and those we hold dear."

Ollie smiled at Priscilla then looked out over the great mass of individuals who now stared with wide eyes and open mouths at the small girl who happened to look a little different. And though they were unable to speak, the citizens of this fragile moon pondered in their own minds what Priscilla had just said.

Suddenly the entire throng of red and blue-haired moon persons, including the kings, felt a tickle in their noses. The tickle grew in intensity, and within seconds it had created an overpowering urge for each person to sneeze. This urge filled each head with an unbelievable pressure. The eyes of citizens and royalty alike bulged, their faces flushed. Then in one, loud, simultaneous release, each person yelled, "Ahh-Ahh-Choo," forcing the mist out of their nostrils.

The fragmented vapors swirled and gathered into one gigantic, dark cloud which now hovered in the sky directly above the castle square. Lightening bolts flashed in all directions across the stratosphere while all waited for the next unpredictable moment.

42

Family Revealed

Their voices restored, the kings wasted no time in responding to the purple-haired child who stood before them.

Norman was the first to rise from his throne. He lifted his nose high in the air and sniffed for a minute or two. Then, seething with an inner rage, he scanned the crowd with his shifty, beady eyes.

"I smell the smell of a traitor," he roared, "for there is only one way to sire a purple-haired kid."

With no words spoken, the senior blue servant went to his daughter and publicly embraced her, but when the pretty red-haired lady made her way up the platform stairs and into Albert's loving arms, there were bewildered gasps of disbelief and near fainting. Confused, the crowd wondered, "Who is this odd-looking threesome?" Albert raised his arms, requesting silence.

"My name is Albert McDoodleNutDoodleMc-Mae," he said in a loud, clear voice. "This is my wife, Willa and this is our daughter, Priscilla, of whom we are most proud."

The mouths of the kings fell open in disbelief while the assembly stood shocked at the blue-haired servant's public acknowledgment of his wife and child.

They began to whisper among themselves.

"Imagine that, a redhead married to a blue haired."

"How odd," some said.

Willa then stepped forward. The crowd hushed again.

"We have lived as a family in isolation for the past 12 years," she said, "but no more. I propose, instead, that we work together to make this moon a home where all citizens can live in peace and harmony, no matter what color of hair they may have."

The kings were speechless once more, completely shocked and angry at this obvious betrayal, but in spite of their reaction, Albert and Willa stood firm, proud of their daughter who now stood between them. There was no turning back.

"Together we can do anything," Willa said, and they joined arms together as one family for all to see.

43

Banished

The kings displayed an instant loathing of the small family who now stood so boldly before them.

"How dare you ask *Why?*" Wynthor roared at Priscilla. "You have disobeyed one of our fundamental laws. Well, kid or no kid, you will be punished for your disobedience."

And to Albert he said, "How dare you betray me? You shall pay the ultimate price for your disloyalty. You are hereby banished from this moon, never to return."

Norman stood next and turned his wrath on Willa.

"You know the law," the red king thundered. "Redheads are not allowed to mix with the inferior blues!"

He stared at her with disgust then continued with his insults.

"No redhead could possibly love a blue-haired person," he shouted. "What a preposterous idea! You are obviously out of your mind, and so I, too, hereby banish you from this moon for all time."

"And you, you wretched baboon," the blue-haired king was now in Ollie's face, "You are a disgrace, and I must be rid of you. Therefore, you are hereby banished and quit holding the hand of that purple-haired freak! I absolutely forbid it!"

But Ollie stood firm, keeping a tight grasp of Priscilla's hand. He would not betray her friendship again.

"This girl is a mistake of nature and of little importance," laughed Norman.

"Whoever heard of a purple-haired person?" Wynthor chimed in. "I agree with Norman. She is a freak, and I will not tolerate her presence any longer."

Priscilla felt the secure hands of her mother and father on her shoulders. The kings' hurtful words were ineffective for she was not alone.

"You are all hereby ordered to leave the premise

immediately," the kings ordered. "Our servants will see you to the gate. There, you will transfer to our sister moon never to return."

"*No!*" spoke a voice that represented every citizen. "The moon belongs to the people! The moon is our home. Let no one take it from us!"

It was the voice of Albert. His day of self-redemption was at hand.

44

In Defiance of
the Kings

Albert and Willa had listened to the kings' taunting long enough. Their cruel words had aroused a justifiable anger within, but instead of retaliating with clenched fists, Albert and Willa, together with their daughter, simply turned their backs. It was an open, direct display of defiance, and it drove the kings to the point of near tantrums. Each royal majesty screamed new orders at their remaining servants.

"Remove these troublemakers at once," they said pointing to Priscilla, and her family. And take that ugly baboon with you. All are traitors. They must leave the premise immediately."

But the royal servants from both sides of the painted lines read the eyes of one another, and then in a single, unified voice responded, "No!" to their majesties' command. They next locked arms along with Ollie and Rodney to form a living shield ready to protect and defend Albert and his family.

Norman and Wynthor stared in disbelief.

"What did you say?" they asked the servants in unison. Both kings were clearly dazed for this was the second time in just a few short minutes that someone had dared to tell them no.

"I believe their answer is no!" Ollie repeated to both kings. The blue baboon stepped forward and continued to address Norman and Wynthor in a loud, clear voice. "I would advise your royal majesties to sit back and listen to someone else speak for a change," and he gave the two kings a nudge that forced them to plop on their velvet thrones tooting as they did so.

Ollie smiled at the wide opened mouth of Rodney.

"Don't look so surprised," the once royal baboon said proudly to the stunned cat. "My *Brave Heart* side has definitely taken control."

Smiling, Rodney stood up on his hind legs. He put his left paw on the shoulder of his new found friend and nodded his head in agreement.

Reenergized, Ollie began to form a new plan of action. "Come with me," he whispered into the royal cat's ear. "I have an idea."

Rodney followed dutifully as the two of them disappeared just inside the castle wall to where open cans of red and blue paint sat in a heap.

"Here we are," Ollie's voice was full of excitement. The brave pet duo then combined the blue paint with the red to form a deep, rich purple color.

"Go to the first and second floor hallways," the baboon ordered Rodney. "Retrieve as many portraits of the kings as you can." The royal cat did as he was told bringing dozens of pictures to where Ollie sat organizing the next step of his brilliant idea. He instructed Rodney on how to print, and then the royal pets proceeded to paint, in purple, the word *Why* across the framed faces of Norman and Wynthor.

Meanwhile the kings were growing extremely nervous.

"I do not trust that crazy baboon with his sensitive rear end," Wynthor said. "He's plotting against me."

"I agree," stated Norman. "We must find our

royal pets so that we can formally banish them along with everyone else."

But when the two kings stood to leave, the unified band of servants prevented their exit.

"We will banish you all," Norman and Wynthor threatened their servants, but a strange new common sense was beginning to enlighten the minds of those there. No longer did the gathered mass of moon people or the kings' servants seem quite as intimidated. Priscilla looked up with pride at her brave father. She watched as he lifted Wynthor's written pledge of allegiance. "I hereby renounce every word in this document," Albert proclaimed in a loud, clear voice. "For it is filled with outright lies and half-truths. Furthermore, no longer will I sit on the side of any king whose selfish ways and policies threaten to destroy the very spirit of my family and fellow citizens.

"In short, my dear Wynthor, I quit!" And he ripped the hand-held document to shreds, tossing the pieces of meaningless paper into the air.

Some of the crowd began to cheer at Albert's open defiance, but the kings took great offense.

They yelled, "Traitors!" and demanded that Albert and his family be taken away, but their words went unheeded for the fate of the moon no longer rested with Norman and Wynthor.

The fate of the moon now rested in the hearts and minds of its own people.

45

Why?

Everything this odd but special family had said made perfect sense. The people listened and conversed. They nodded in quiet, respectful debate and then conversed some more. There was much hubbub as the royal pets distributed *Why* painted portraits to the moon's gathered citizens.

"*Why* can't we live without lines that divide?" asked a blue-haired lady holding her sign up for all to see.

"*Why* is purple hair wrong?" rang out a voice from a different corner of the square.

"And *Why* can't all colors of hair get along?" questioned another.

Then, like a giant wave taking hold, others held high their signs while chanting, "*Why*?"

"Stop!" screamed Norman and Wynthor. The

two crazy kings covered their ears but the voice of the people would not be silenced. The REDS and the BLUES were demanding change, and their voices grew *louder*, and *louder* and *louder* till it became a deafening roar that caused the moon surface to quake and the mysterious dark cloud to descend. The cloud swirled out of control unleashing a strange kind of power.

Whirling gusts engulfed the tiny moon, hurling and tossing all those still divided by the painted lines. Citizens flew in every direction; no one escaped. The colored sand was loosened and the moon tremors increased in intensity. The blowing sand soon covered each and every person.

The moon inhabitants had no understanding of the power set free. Everyone was at the mercy of the wind. They extended their hands and attempted to reach for each other with no regard for one another's color of hair. But the wind in its fury would not allow anyone to grab hold. Each citizen was alone in this great storm and amid the panic they came to an important realization; they needed one another, the RED and the BLUE, the large and the small, the young and the old.

"It's the end of our world," cried several voices, and Priscilla wondered if indeed the moon's final day was at hand.

The wind carried the brave purple-haired girl like a feather on a soft, billowy cloud high above the square. Yet, unlike most of her fellow citizens, she was not afraid.

She closed her eyes and surrendered once again to the Presence, revealed this time, in the awesome power of the wind.

46

The Conversion

Suddenly, the quaking ceased, and the powerful wind that had reeled its fury just a moment before was absorbed into the clear blue sky above. It left the moon citizens bewildered and frightened.

All was quiet. The painted lines had split from one end of the moon to the other leaving cracks in its surface.

"What did this mean?" The people wondered. "Where do we go from here? What does the future hold?"

There were no answers. Then in the stillness, a voice full of hope broke the silence. It was the voice of the old clock maker.

"What a mess," he called out in an excited voice. "What a wonderful mixed up mess."

The wind had left him hanging high off the

roof of his little shop. From there he had a terrific view of the square below. He looked down and gazed at the incredible sight. Some of the reds and the blues found themselves together on doorsteps. Some folks twirled on weather vanes and others sat on fence posts. Some were left on rooftops and some on steeples. The two kings, quite symbolically, dangled from flag poles. But most citizens were left lying on the ground of the great square, their hair and clothes spattered with red and blue sand.

Priscilla, who had drifted higher than anyone, was gently let down by an unknown Presence into the arms of her mother and father. They stood together safe at last, and the fear and isolation that had once dominated their lives was now replaced with open freedom and a wonderful sense of belonging.

The moon was indeed a royal mess. Carts were turned over and pieces of *Why* signs were strewn everywhere. But the wise old timekeeper saw only the blessing in the disarray that lay before them. He viewed their present situation as a tremendous opportunity to rebuild their moon together.

Then Mr. Zotter did something that no one had

done in a very long time; he laughed. And the sound of his laughter spread to all corners of the square and beyond. Soon the entire moon was filled with elated citizens. Their laughter, mixed with cheers and applause, grew into a tidal wave of uncontrollable joy. They were wonderfully bewildered, unsure of the meaning of what had just happened but certain to start life anew, each and every person respectful of one another.

And they rose up ready to work for the common good, confident that a new moon would rise from the destruction because the hearts of a people had changed.

"Your hair is beautiful," said a blue-haired lady working close to Priscilla.

"Yes, very beautiful," came the voice of another, and her children alongside her agreed.

47

The Return

At last the long, historical day was over. Exhausted, both mentally and physically, all citizens returned to their homes for a much needed rest. They promised to return the next day and for many days after. Together, they would build a better moon, a moon that would reflect the unique gifts and talents of all the good citizens who resided there.

It was an exciting concept and one that Albert felt deserved serious consideration. But now his mind was tired. He longed for his own warm bed and a night of undisturbed sleep.

Priscilla and Willa had returned to their cottage a short while ago. Albert had promised to join them soon.

Wynthor and Norman had retired to their chambers at a much earlier hour. It had been a very shocking day for them. Both kings, it was agreed, could stay a few nights longer in the castle until other homes were found for them. However, it was understood that their time of self-serving government was over. Decisions made by the people would now set in motion new laws that would hopefully guide and lead all the moon's citizens in a just and meaningful way.

Albert stood in the square and briefly recalled the day's events. He did not notice the silhouette of a meek-looking woman standing alone in the twilight till he was ready to leave. She appeared frightened, as if she wanted to run and hide, and yet something held her back. He began walking toward her and then recognized her face. It was the old fish lady who had bribed him the day before.

She wore the same drab, gray dress with the fish-stained apron, but her attitude had changed. She stood quietly, her hands behind her back.

"Can I help you?" Albert asked in a caring voice.

The fish lady began to shake, her eyes welling with tears. She seemed sad and deeply troubled.

Albert watched as she slowly reached into her

apron pocket. She hesitated for a moment then pulled out her clenched hand. Without a word the fish lady placed the precious gift within Albert's open palm closing his fingers around it.

"I believe," she said, with her head humbly bowed, "that this belongs to you. Please know how very sorry I am." And with that, she was gone.

Albert opened his hand and read the inscription etched on the inside cover of his anniversary watch.

"*One day,*" he said aloud, and his heart was filled with a new sense of hope and gratitude for not only this day but for all the days yet to come.

Be good to your neighbor.

Show others you care.

Speak kindly.

Rejoice with all colors of hair.

Make peace as you journey

So all understand

That life is more fun

Without lines in the sand.

Part Six

(One Year Later)

And since that great day, most who live on this moon

Including one special, brave smiling baboon

Have learned in their homes, in their cities and schools

To learn and uphold these important moon rules:

Be good to your neighbor. Show others you care.

Speak kindly. Rejoice with all colors of hair.

Make peace as you journey so all understand

That life is more fun without lines in the sand.

48

A New Life

News of the moon rules had spread quickly to those living on other celestial bodies. A steady stream of curious visitors came to see this new way of life in action.

All was well. Minds remained open, and ears stopped to listen. As a result, all citizens grew in mind and heart. The moon now was a kaleidoscope of all colors and sizes and ages. Life was good.

Beautiful flowers and trees now grew where the red and blue lines had once been painted. Quaint, little bridges allowed all colors of hair to pass from one side of the square to the other. There were clean streams of flowing water and playgrounds with picnic tables. Ice cream and soda shops were intermingled with other places of business.

Uplifting songs now played through the

loudspeakers. A colorful, new roof overhung the platform where the former kings had once sat on ruby and sapphire thrones. It was now a stage for celebrating different ways of different cultures. There were concerts and theater presentations and fun gatherings for all to enjoy.

Everyone said, "Please" and "Thank you."

And soon they discovered that each and every person born into this life does indeed have the power to make a difference.

It was time to celebrate. The governing council proclaimed a national holiday.

Priscilla, Ollie and Rodney served as greeters at the great castle gate. Everyone was invited to this giant celebration including Norman and Wynthor, but they had chosen to stay away.

Priscilla thought back to that fateful day one year ago. Much had been accomplished, but there were still miles to go. She was ever so grateful for the ties that had formed. Those ties, she knew would only grow stronger as time went on.

She was especially grateful for Ollie, for he had become a true and reliable friend. She had a gift for him on this one-year anniversary. She pulled him aside and in a sincere, simple voice said, "Thank you for your gift of friendship."

Ollie was caught off guard. "Awe shucks, Priscilla," he said. He unwrapped his gift and then smiled at the sight of a brand new silver harmonica. "You remembered," Ollie said.

Then from the crowd he heard a familiar voice.

"Hello, Ollie, my dear."

He looked to the plump, blue-haired, lady baboon standing directly in front of him.

"Mama," he whispered.

49

Reunited at Last

Joyful tears flowed down the cheeks of Ollie's mother.

"It's all right, Mama," Ollie's father kept repeating while drying his own eyes.

She finally relinquished the hold on her son only to have him devoured by the arms of his father and a multitude of adopted brothers and sisters who kept calling him Bro. Each new, colorful sibling, though from a different species, wore the same genuine smile. Ollie sensed their joyful acceptance of him. "Together we make quite a handsome group," he thought.

"These children were orphaned on our sister moon," Ollie's mother explained. "They had no family to care for them,"

She looked deep into the tearful eyes of her

son, "My heart was broken the day we were separated, and so your father and I decided to take in these beautiful, orphaned babes of the wood. They were captured like you but banished because of their different colors of hair. We have since grown into a loving, close-knit family and now we are complete.

"This is the happiest day of my life." And she threw her arms once more around Ollie and cried some more.

"Mama," said Ollie's father, "introduce your son to his new family."

"Oh, yes, of course. "Ollie, these are your sisters, Ellie, Maddie, Gabbie, Molly, Maggie, Ruby, Sylvie and Callie.

"And these are your new brothers, Ethan, Murray, Max, Gavin, Gibson, Mason and Brody."

Priscilla stood back and watched with tearful eyes.

"There is a story spreading across the entire galaxy," said Ollie's father to his son, "that you and a young girl named Priscilla helped to de-throne your former kings."

"Why, yes we did," chimed in Ollie. "It was

quite the battle. I had to resort to physical tactics like judo and karate using my bare hands to keep others safe. It was unbelievable."

"Yes, quite unbelievable," Priscilla said with a slight grin

"Is this the Priscilla we've been told about?" Ollie's mom asked in a warm tone while turning toward the pretty purple-haired girl standing next to her.

"Why, yes it is, Mama. She's also my dearest friend. Look at what she just gave me," and he ran his lips along his new harmonica.

"Hot diggity-dog!" yelled Ollie's father. "You're just what we need to complete our band."

They all carried their own musical instrument. There was a look of excitement on each of the adopted faces.

"We have formed a little musical group called the *MOLINKA MANIACS*," said Ollie's father. "And if you don't mind my saying so, we can really bring the house down with our own unique style."

"You must perform tonight at our moon celebration," Priscilla insisted.

"Absolutely!" Ollie cried out. "Let's rock 'n roll!"

Then, with arms embraced they all proceeded to the platform in the square.

It wasn't till the Molinkas left the gate that Priscilla saw a tall, older gentleman watching and waiting patiently.

"May I help you?" she inquired.

"Why, yes, I believe you can," he said. "I would very much like to speak with your father, please."

"And whom shall I say is calling?" Priscilla asked.

"Tell him the Reverend Thomas T. Tooker respectfully requests the pleasure of his company."

THE END START OF A
BRAND NEW BEGINNING

ABOUT THE AUTHOR

Ten years ago, Janet Mary Sinke was diagnosed with Parkinson's Disease. This illness caused her to embark upon a new career, that of author and publisher. Formerly a hospice nurse for many years, she became the creator of the *Grandma Janet Mary* Series.

This series of award-winning picture books, are all written in rhyme and center on the grandchild-grandparent relationship. She regards her grandchildren as her main source of inspiration but views her own health challenges as inspirational, also.

> *"Strange as it may seem, my Parkinson's is one of my greatest blessings, for it has led me down a road I would have otherwise never traveled. This road has allowed me to view life from a whole new perspective, and for that I am eternally grateful."*

Then, three years ago, in the middle of the night, a different story emerged from the pen of this talented author titled:

Priscilla McDoodleNutDoodleMcMae Asks Why?

It is considered by many to be her best work. Written in wonderful, whimsical rhyme, this tale of transformation is meant for all ages, for it calls upon each of us to make a difference in our world. The success of the Priscilla story in picture-book form stimulated this author to develop further the characters of this award-winning book. Two years later, this chapter book titled

Priscilla Asks Why? The Rest of the Story

is now ready to share. Together we can make a difference.

Make peace as you journey
So all understand
That life is more fun without
Lines in the sand.

Janet Mary Sinke continues to battle Parkinson's. The disease, though progressing, has not hindered her spirit. She remains committed to the message of Priscilla and to any meaningful story that promotes peace and understanding.

Her next goal: to make Priscilla into an animated film.

"We shall see where the Spirit leads."

Janet Mary Sinke is mother to five children and grandmother to 15. She resides in St. Johns, Michigan with her husband, Mike.

Other Titles By Janet Mary Sinke

I Wanna Go to Grandma's House
ISBN: 0-9742732-0-1
Ben Franklin Award—Gold Recipient
Mom's Choice Award—Gold Recipient

Grandma's Christmas Tree
ISBN: 0-9742732-1-X

Grandpa's Fishin' Friend
ISBN: 0-9742732-2-8
Ben Franklin Award—Gold Recipient
Mom's Choice Award—Gold Recipient

Grandma's Treasure Chest
ISBN: 0-974732-3-6
Ben Franklin Award—Silver Recipient
Mom's Choice Award—Gold Recipient

My Grandpa's Coaching Third
ISBN-13: 978-0-9742732-5-9
Children's Moonbeam Award—Silver Recipient

Priscilla McDoodleNutDoodleMcMae, Asks Why?
ISBN-13: 978-0-9742732-8-0
Children's Moonbeam Award—Gold Recipient
Mom's Choice Award—Gold Recipient
Eric Hoffer Award—1st Place—Children's Category

Ten Lessons Learned Gifts from those Remembered
ISBN-13: 978-0-9742732-4-2
(Meditative/Self help)
Mom's Choice Award—-Gold Recipient

To purchase;
check with local book stores
order online: www.mygrandmaandme.com
or call direct at 989-224-4078